The God Dichotomy

Hans Benes

Publisher's Cataloging-in-Publication data

Names: Benes, Hans, author.
Title: The God dichotomy / Hans Benes.
Description: Includes bibliographical references. | Parker, CO: Hans Benes, 2021.
Identifiers: ISBN: 978-1-950647-95-8
Subjects: LCSH Benes, Hans--Fiction. | Spirituality--Fiction. | God--Fiction. |
BISAC FICTION / Biographical | FICTION / Religious |
FICTION / Visionary & Metaphysical
Classification: LCC PS3602.E46565 G63 2021 | DDC 813.6--dc23

Publishing assistance by BookCrafters, Parker, CO
www.bookcrafters.net

"There is no science that can identify God;
there is no philosophy that can define God.
God cannot be explained;
God can only be experienced."

"So you want to experience God?
It's quite simple: do good,
be good, in everything you say and do,
without exception!"

—Hans Benes from Spirit

Acknowledgements

I would be remiss not to acknowledge those individuals who played an integral part in both my spiritual growth and in helping me publish this lifelong project. No one can travel the life journey without a helping hand or encouragement from someone, whether it is a family member, a friend or a complete stranger. Support often comes in strange and mysterious ways.

A very special thank you is due to Ruth Stoner who lit the fires of spirituality within me through her New Age insight of the Divine. It was through Ruth's insight I began to meditate. It was with her assistance I began to look internally for spiritual growth. Had Ruth not entered my life I would, quite possibly, still be looking outward to find God.

I also want to thank my writing group, Mimi Normile, Lynn Haass, Pat Karam and Jim Vander Kamp, whose support and encouragement to continue writing were instrumental in publishing *From Danzig to New York*, which led directly to this project. We all attended the Academy for Lifelong Learning and formed our writing group once our class ended. They were the inspiration to the characters depicted herein.

A very special thank you to Dr. Vern Martin whose spiritual messages have resonated within me for some time. His encouragement to follow my passion of writing was instrumental in overcoming the demon of procrastination that kept my opinion and beliefs silent for far too long.

Dr. Vern's repeated message of spiritual love and brotherhood have become the cornerstone of my belief system.

Nothing, however, would have been possible without the support of my wife, Jannette. As a Science of Mind Practitioner (RScP) she has helped me forage through various religious and spiritual dogmas and teaching by keeping me focused on my personal growth. Her daily prayers for family, friends and me have helped numerous people meet and overcome hardships. She truly understands the power of prayer. Without her, none of this would have been possible.

Introduction

We are all on a journey, a journey called life. We enter life with nothing and we leave it the same way. In between there is nothing but window dressing, events and happenings we deem necessary to ensure a successful and meaningful existence. By developing our own, biased filters we embark through life with visions of successes and triumphs. Each event, however, takes us further from the truth, further from who we really are.

Unfortunately, our journey is never about individualized gain. Our journey is never about the ascension of power. Our journey is never about fostering success at the behest of another. Our journey is, quite simply, an awakening to who we really are.

There are many, many roads on this journey and no two paths are alike. We have the freedom to choose where to go, when to go and how to get there. We have freedom to create, to love and to live our truth.

While our journey through life is filled with adventure, set backs and criticism, both positive and negative, our journey through life is, nevertheless, a testament to who we are individually and collectively. Obstacles lay before us waiting to ensnare us in a malaise of fear and doubt. Some of us work through these hurdles, learning and enriching our lives in the process. Others, however, become entrenched in life's imperfections and view them as personal shortcomings.

How we face these issues and deal with them on a daily basis is the crux of what life is all about. Life, quite frankly, is a mask hiding our very spiritual nature from us. Spirituality rarely offers tangible results and is, therefore, easily dismissed in a material world. Our world of humanity is primarily senses driven and what can't be seen, touched or heard is easily dismissed as supernatural. God is such an enigma.

How life unfolds for us is determined by our internal, intangible system of beliefs and desires. Therein lies our true dichotomy: our tangible world is driven by intangible values and beliefs. Including God, with all of the spiritual tenets and expectancies, further clouds the life journey. It's little wonder most people engage life from a fear based perspective having its roots in a history of struggle and failure. It appears only a select few are granted the "keys to the kingdom" while the majority toil in daily occupations to make ends meet.

But what happens when we include God in our daily activities? Does His inclusion create a more demanding existence for us or does He offer insights often overlooked or misunderstood? It is a decision not easily embraced. Our roller coaster of life rarely slows down to allow us the wherewithal to ponder and analyze what life is placing in our path. It is often less intrusive to forge ahead on our life journey without the comfort and support of God. God, it seems, adds another layer of reality to a life filled with material demands, which call out to us on a daily basis demanding to be heard. Spirituality then becomes this enigma waiting patiently to be incorporated in our life journey; all too often it never is.

So how do we come to terms with a deity looking to be included in our lives while living in a system based on material results? Juggling these seemingly opposing systems with their fraught expectancies becomes a major task not everyone is willing to entertain. And those that do often find themselves at odds as established rules for religion and society become diametrically opposed. It seems easier to submit to the status quo of both systems than to challenge the veracity of either one. Life all too often follows a trek countless others have embarked upon before us.

Is this journey what life is all about, or is there more to it than we realize? Who are we, really? Rarely do we stop the merry-go-round of life to ask these questions; rarely do we have the time. But when we do, we often come up with enlightened answers. Is our journey a materialistic or spiritual one? Could it be both simultaneously? Most important, however, is whether this life is all there is! Coming to grasps with these questions is a basic precursor to who we really are and understanding our purpose in life.

My existence is a sojourn in a physical world intent on creating a reality from which there is no escape. My ego driven belief system continues to prioritize day to day living in a competitive and results driven environment. Who has time for spirituality when the immediate needs demand to be satisfied? I grew up in a household of need where food, clothing and security dominated the survival system. God and spirit were ideals dismissed long ago, while hard work was prioritized as a precursor to success.

As I grew, I began to absorb these same ideals my parents taught me. I began to look at my life and saw only tangible needs and success. Raising children and maintaining a respectable living environment was enabled by a well-entrenched financial system that dictated success or failure. God was an afterthought.

It was only through modest success and one tragic loss that I focused on more intangible necessities. Money and all the wealth on this planet could not remedy my loss. But God did offer one thing: a calming of anxiety and, more importantly, a promise of a better tomorrow. There was, it seems, something to be embraced in the intangible world of Spirit. But understanding and doing are quite opposites and continue to fight for supremacy over an abject mind ill prepared for the conflict.

So how does one prepare for the internal struggle between mind and matter? The ego, I learned, does not submit easily. Its grip on this material world is real and powerful. It scoffs at thoughts and ideas failing to bring food to the table or keeping a roof over one's head. It continually plays the need and success card that obliterates anything it feels counterproductive to tangible goals. This journey is never easy and rarely encounters a smooth and well-paved road.

Join me on my journey that is far from over and will, in all likelihood, continue throughout my lifetime. I have chosen to question my internal appeasement of a world with predetermined expectancies reliant on self-serving accomplishments. I have chosen to think with my heart, exhibiting compassion and empathy to my neighbors. I have come to believe the masses can accomplish far more than any individual. Yet breaking the chains of individualism is nearly impossible in a world dominated by "mine" and "yours."

Herein is my journey.

Here I Stand

Here I stand,
On the precipice of greatness,
Where riches and fame and notoriety await.
All it takes is a step.
But here I stand,
Entrenched.
Entrenched in a life of need and fear.
Entrenched in beliefs and values not my own.
Where hope of escape, escapes me,
Where hope of change is a long, lost dream,
Of sugar plums and gifts long replaced
By the needs of everyday living.
Where making money is a judgment
Of success.
Where philanthropy is a sign of compassion
And spirituality.
Yes, here I stand filled with emotions
Urging me forward to an unknown place,
Not one established by a society blinded
By eons of messages of worthlessness and subservience.

Yet, here I stand,
On the precipice of greatness.
Do I dare to follow my heart In directions unknown,
Through hills and valleys filled with burdens
Where greatness is measured by strength of heart?
Do I have the resolve necessary
To become the next Lincoln or Gandhi or Buddha?

When my little sister says I stink.
Is it a self imposed doubt and fear of failure
That saps my courage and sense of adventure?

I close my eyes to dream the impossible dream.
And I hear Dr. Martin Luther King proclaim,
"I have a dream!"
It all begins with a vision,
An idea easily dismissed.
But it lingers.
It stays within you night and day.
It says, "Yes! You can do it as have many before you."
It says, "Yes! You are just as good as any of them.
The only difference is they took that step."

So take that step!
Take the step so you may live and bask in the experience.
Take the step to erase all those doubts and fears
That have resided in the catacombs of your mind
For far too long.
The next step you take
Will change your life!
You only need to decide whether it be forward or backward.
One step from the precipice of greatness.
Yes, here I stand!

Table of Contents

Chapter - 1

Is That God?

"Religion encourages you to explore the thoughts of others and accept them as your own. Spirituality invites you to toss away the thoughts of others and come up with your own."
—Neale Donald Walsch

"Is that God?"

The young voice pierced through the quiet house of worship like the cracking of a lightning bolt, temporarily startling the priest in his flowing robe entering the altar area. Parishioners were jerked out of their personal prayers and those whose meditative journey took them too deeply were rudely awakened. All eyes, synchronized in unwitting unison, turned to the back of the sanctuary searching for the source of the unwelcomed interruption. As if on cue, the organ began to divert everyone's attention to the task at hand as the melodious "Beautiful Savior" replaced the unsolicited distraction.

Taken aback by the sudden attention, my aunt hastily whispered "No," while placing her index finger over her puckered lips. While some chuckled discreetly, most of the worshippers had risen and turned their attention to the popular hymn by joining the priest in singing the first two verses.

Not being able to see above the standing congregation, my frustrated sister moved around incessantly trying to see what was going on. As the song came to an end and everyone sat, she remained standing to ensure a better glimpse of what would happen next. She did, to my aunt's delight, remain silent although her movement occasionally interrupted the sanctity of the moment. Every once in a while she discreetly whispered into my aunt's ear, "What is he doing?" A stern look would generally be returned and my sister would remain still for another five minutes.

"Was that embarrassing!" is all my Aunt Trautchen could say as they returned home. She had to laugh, however, at the inquisitiveness of her six-year-old niece and how they somehow managed to stay for the entire service. My sister even got to shake the priest's hand while properly curtseying, receiving a well-intentioned smile in return.

I listened intently, not wanting to miss anything my aunt or sister had to say. For me, it was the first time someone I was close to had, actually stepped inside the Catholic Church on Eupenerstrasse in Bremerhaven, Germany. I had walked past the church frequently and always saw it as the place where God lived. Having been told He was always watching and judging people, it was a place I wasn't eager to visit.

Echoing in my mind was my sister's impression of the vastness inside the church and how impossible it was to remember everything she saw. Likewise, God was also this vast individual who was incomprehensible to this young spiritual novice. He remained invisible yet saw everything everyone did; He was loving and kind yet punished those who misbehaved; and He expected to hear prayers yet rarely answered them for people in need. God was an enigma, especially to a young boy who could barely fathom the world of materialism.

It was my mother who first introduced me to a Higher Power by quoting my grandfather, an avowed Communist, "You don't have to go to church to believe in God." At the time this insight meant little to a young boy more intent on playing and getting into trouble than worrying about the meaning of God and religion. To me, God was this ever-present figure, high above, watching everyone to make sure people would do what they were supposed to and punish the ones who did not. God was a figure to be feared, a judge who determined people's fate in deciding who would go to heaven and who would burn in the fires of hell.

Everything had now changed for me. God was no longer someone far away on some distant star or planet, he was right down the street, just a couple of blocks away and my sister had seen him. More than that, she shook his hand. From what I could tell, he was friendly enough and I vowed to be on my best behavior lest he come to look and punish me for some misdeed. More importantly for me, here was all the proof I needed that God actually existed.

My sister rudely interrupted my thoughts, "There were a lot of prayers. People were asking for all kinds of things. Mom, does God answer prayers?"

"Yes," came a somewhat hesitant reply.

"So if I ask God for something he'll give it to me?"

Mom's face seemed to sadden as her eyes became watery to a point where a single tear traced its tracks along her cheek, "God has been known to answer prayers."

I didn't think much about my mom's reply until years later when, much older and wiser, the journey of a single tear began to make sense to me. In the wake of 45 million lost lives there must have been countless prayers sent heavenward by millions of people asking for the wellbeing of loved ones and food to sustain them for another day while pleading that today's bombs would not destroy their homes or the lives of friends and family. My grandfather lost a brother, my father lost a brother and my mom lost a sister. There wasn't a family in Europe unaffected by the carnage of World War II.

What kind of God would allow this to happen? What kind of God would stand by and watch the senseless slaughter of people and destruction of their homes? What kind of God would turn a blind eye to the pleading prayers of millions who were at the great abyss of life asking themselves, "Will I still be alive tomorrow?"

A simple question by a six-year old girl had somehow opened deep emotional and psychological scars my mom worked hard to conceal. I could finally understand her perception of God as a superior being who just didn't care about the wellbeing of good and decent people enduring unimaginable pain and distress. Such a being, which stood for everything good and loving, could not possibly stand idly by and let this happen. He didn't protect her from beatings administered by a strict and demanding father, nor did he protect her from the atrocities and callousness of war. A god who condones such actions could not possibly exist.

Time had become too precious to waste on words of hope; survival required one's total attention. If she were to survive it would be by using her own inner strength and guile, not by uttering senseless prayers. God either couldn't care less or didn't exist, what did it matter? Tomorrow was not guaranteed nor did it promise to alleviate the suffering. Instead, prayers for safety and security often turned into requests for a swift and painless death.

Days turned into weeks and weeks into months and months into years. Lives were lost and destroyed, homes bombed out and hope lost in the sanctity of an uncaring deity. Yes, it was a lot easier to dismiss the goodness of God and, better yet, it became less painful to think he didn't exist at all.

God was, almost, non-existent during those early years of my childhood. No one in our family circle paid any mind to any deity. Survival was paramount as food, clothing and shelter were priorities that circumvented the need for God. Monthly tithes, in the form of a church tax, were automatically deducted from paychecks; it was a steep price to pay to ensure the continuation of His church that appeared to be more absorbed with its own survival. God didn't lend a hand, but it seems, his acolytes surely held their hands out.

Yet for some inconceivable reason my mother felt it necessary to have my sister and myself baptized. We were about six or seven when a priest visited my grandfather's house to christen his newly born son, my uncle. I can only assume it was his new wife who insisted in her son's cleansing of original sin; a devout Communist's tolerance and belief in Holy Sacraments seems implausible. I certainly wasn't aware of the significance of the event, nor did I understand the meaning of this Christian ritual. It felt awkward to have water anoint my head for a reason I didn't comprehend. At least I didn't cry like my uncle did. Totally unaware of the spiritual purification baptism provided, I was now, nonetheless, eligible to enter through the gates of heaven and bask in everlasting bliss. More importantly, this Holy Sacrament did not transform my world nor did it change my daily ritual. Being forgiven by God for my sins meant little to a boy whose priorities lay in a material world fraught with obstacles and problems.

As the years passed, God was rarely on my mind and talked about even less in our family circle. Hard work and saving for a better tomorrow became the prevailing ideal. It was up to my parents to forge a future, God was nothing more than an inconsequential bystander. In Karl Marx's view, "Religious suffering is, at one and the same time, the expression of real suffering and a protest against real suffering. Religion is the sigh of the oppressed creature, the heart of a heartless world, and the soul of soulless conditions. It is the opium of the people." My grandfather's acceptance of the Communist ideal had, unwittingly and unknowingly undermined any hope for our family's spiritual acceptance.

When leaving Bremerhaven on that fateful day in September 1955, I not only left my dear family, but also an uncaring and self-serving deity. I did not know it at the time, but I was immigrating to a country built on political and religious freedom. It was the bright lights of an always busy New York City, appearing daunting and overwhelming, that welcomed me to my new home. Its Statue of Liberty standing as a symbol of personal freedom could not be ignored. God was aboard the *T.S.S. New York* that day to ensure a safe and uneventful crossing of the Atlantic; I just wasn't aware of it.

Chapter – 2

He's Gone

"But I am only death. I am not the end of all existence, only the one you know. In fact, I really do not exist; I am a concept which mankind has invented because they lack the knowledge and understanding beyond the physical world. Therein lies my noumenon; I am death, not the terminator of life, as you would believe, but the terminator of time. I take your future and erase your past and embrace you in an everlasting present."

—Spirit

"He's gone!"
"What do you mean he's gone?"
"He's gone! Johnny's dead!"

It was January 2, 2015 around 11 P.M., a time when phone calls usually bring ominous tidings. Nothing good, it seems, ever comes from a late night call. This was worse, it was my personal Pearl Harbor, a day that will forever live in infamy.

After Jannette's shocking announcement I sat stunned trying to digest what I just heard. My mind was in hyper drive and super slow speed, all at the same time. It went backwards and forwards trying to make sense of it all. I heard Jannette crying in the background; but for me, the tears didn't come as they were held back by a dam of stoicism, fighting mightily to refuse to process or comprehend the information just given. I sat staring, not focusing on anything specific, for what seemed like an eternity.

My senses failed to react to any stimuli as my current state was controlled by internal emotions, or lack thereof. One never knows how one will react to extraordinary circumstance under extreme duress; suffice it to say there are no standard responses to sudden tragic events. Questions seemed to dominate my cerebral dialogue. Why? How? When? Where?

Yet beyond them all was the inescapable hope somehow someone had gotten it all wrong. I held on to the slightest hope of doubt for as long as I possibly could.

"It's not Johnny, it's someone else."

This recurring message became an automatic response to any thought of the inevitable. This response stayed the emotional roller coaster threatening to crash at any moment. Through it all, the eyes remained dry, afraid a singular blink would recognize my emotional weakness by releasing an unrestrained flood of tears. After countless minutes I felt obligated to inform my eldest son, Christopher, of the tragic news. That he answered his phone this late at night was surprising as well.

"Hello?"

"I have some terrible news."

"What is it?"

"Johnny's dead."

There was a stark silence at the other end of the phone as Chris, I assumed, was trying to understand what I was telling him. During the wait I felt emotions rising through my body, threatening to explode momentarily. I fought back the welling tears and managed to conclude our conversation. "I don't have any information. I'll let you know as soon as I hear anything. I have to go."

"OK."

I hung up and continued my staring, hoping to clear my tear-filled eyes. Stopping the tears, however, didn't stop the sinus cavities from filling up and exert a baseball size knot in the middle of my face.

No one is immune to personal emotions, and no matter how hard one tries, the dam will burst eventually. Finally, I turned my eyes heavenward and asked, "God, why have you forsaken me? Why did this have to be?" Like my mother's prayers 70 years earlier, there were no answers and I was left standing alone for what seemed like an eternity, held up by some invisible force while cement shoes bonded me to the floor.

Sleep did not come easy that night as thoughts, memories and questions raced through the hollow hallways of my mind. Emotions rose and fell as an occasional single tear silently traced my cheek and fell to be absorbed by my pillow. It was a night filled with a runny nose and an aching heart as I tried in vain to make sense of it all.

What pained most, however, was the missed opportunity to speak with him personally. My last contact with Johnny was a text conversation resulting from my Christmas message, "Merry Christmas. Thinking about you. Hope all is well."

After twenty minutes the reply came, "Who's this?"

I did not know how to take this, whether it was sarcasm or if someone else was replying for him. It took another two hours for a follow up message to arrive.

"Merry Christmas to you! All is not! Have you ever felt completely alone, lost everything you've ever worked hard for, every time you think your pulling your ass outta the shit everything falls apart, hopeless and broken? That's me! Thanks for thinking and hopefully you feel better about anything bad you're dealing with! Well then, until the next time you think! Cheerio!"

I pondered this response for a while, not knowing exactly what to think or where he was coming from. I did, unfortunately, feel the pain and call for help, or so I thought. After 45 minutes I responded.

"Yes, I've been there. Fortunately I had caring people to talk to, both personally and professionally. With their help I learned that my self-worth was critical in my recovery. I learned to forge my own truth, not anyone else's. By doing so I built a life of forgiveness and happiness, without regret. I learned to feel good about myself and that was the most important lesson. Losing all possessions is meaningless; losing your self-esteem is critical. There are plenty of people that care about you. If you want to talk. call me."

It was our last contact. It was also the first exchange in about six months, a time marred with angry words and emotional outbursts leaving us both, I'm sure, physically and psychologically spent. It re-opened a chasm in our relationship that would never be repaired.

Were the words in his final text a call for help? I believe so. My lingering question remains, would I have been better off calling him rather than texting him? He had, long ago, indicated his preferred method of communicating with me was via text messaging, as the vast majority of my calls went unanswered and, since his voice mailbox was eternally full, a message could never be left. Was this another case where hurt feelings dictated an improper response? It is a decision I will question for a long time. But for now I have to prepare to bury my son.

There were three deaths actually, all in succession. First to leave this earthly realm was my son-in-law John's stepfather, followed the next day by his mother. While those deaths were not unexpected they did little to prepare anyone for the shocking news to come.

With the Wyoming losses still fresh on their minds, our daughter, Dianah, rushed back to Colorado requesting we make her a reservation for the somber trip to New York. My son Paul would fly in from San Diego and meet us in New York. On Monday, January 5th, fresh off a New Years celebration, we boarded a Southwest flight bound for La Guardia. Christopher and his family made arrangements to fly to New York via Jet Blue.

There had already been a myriad of activity including Joey and Michael, Johnny's uncles, identifying the body in the morgue. Funeral arrangements were made to the request and approval of his mother, Lynn. While I felt my son's funeral should be a quiet and simple affair that, however, was not as his mother saw it. I didn't argue the point. I had yet to cry.

Upon our arrival in New York, we headed straight to my granddaughters' house. Johnny's daughters, along with their mother Michelle, were going through photographs scattered over the dining room table, as they were busy creating a storyboard of their father's life for placement in the funeral home. As is always the case, each photograph brought back memories of days gone by often permeating a feeling of melancholy within the room. Many tears were brushed aside while my eyes remained dry. The uncomfortable baseball in my face would not, however, go away.

Although I recognized the surrounding pictures, the face of the body lying in the coffin only looked vaguely familiar. It had a waxy look, devoid of all emotion and energy. It was an empty shell I used to call my son. It was only when I noticed a fragment of a tattoo peeking from the sleeve of his suit that I came to accept this was, indeed, Johnny. Filled with flowers and Catholic religious symbols of various types, the hall purported to be a sanctuary depicting a high degree of spirituality. To me it seemed unacceptable that God would make His presence known here when He could have made a dramatic difference had He surfaced just a few days earlier. What happened to eternal, unconditional love?

I looked around at familiar faces that were, for a long time, central to both of our lives. While I had moved on, Johnny had not and remained a focal member of my ex wife's family. Many eyes were reddened with tears while mine remained dry, still trying to make sense of it all. The why, how and what kept reemerging in my mind like Yellowstone's Old Faithful, followed quickly by thoughts hoping this wasn't really happening, it's all one big dream or rather, a nightmare. Somewhere there had to be a logical explanation for all of this.

It's impossible to explain how thoughts keep racing through the mind while the moments in time appear to move in slow motion. The inevitable consolations began slowly as a line of well-wishers and consolers slowly grew. When I turned from the coffin it felt like a hundred pairs of eyes were watching me, waiting for my emotional breakdown. Still I did not cry, remaining stoic through it all.

THE GOD DICHOTOMY

My eyes strain to see beyond the blackness.
My ears perk at diminutive sounds.
As a frigid wind strokes my face
Behind these cold, gray bars.

I see a blue and white orb,
Surrounded by darkness,
While faint lights strain in the background
As I peer beyond these cold, gray bars.

Yesterday is but a memory
And tomorrow will never appear
In my contemporary world,
Behind these cold, gray bars.

I think about what might have been,
For fear of going insane;
Passion is a pain quickly absorbed
By these cold, gray bars.

The emptiness of my womb
Cascades throughout my flesh,
While my child
Is lost in life's great abyss.

Beyond is the great rainbow,
A spectacle of blacks and grays;
With promises of a darkened sun
For yet another day.

As melancholy spirits abound
In this house without a soul,
Where dampness chills me to the bone,
I'm a prisoner within my mind.

Slowly I raise my head
And let out a sigh.
As another tear runs down my cheek
Rusting away my cold, gray bars.

Will life ever get back to normal or will this personal malaise continue, for who knows how long? Sorrow, I have found, does not necessarily begin and end with tears. More often than not it manifests itself with periods of depression and regret. What could I have done? Why didn't I do something? Could it have been prevented? My self-inflicted emotional pain buried my need for spiritual peace deep within my psyche. God may not have played a hand in my son's suicide, but then, He apparently didn't see a need to prevent it either.

Death, in itself, is a hard pill to swallow. But when it comes knocking unexpectedly on your door because someone close and dear has decided to end their life in one tragic, bewildering act, it brings forth a stampede of emotional turmoil: sadness, sorrow, guilt and anger amongst them. I, however, remained stoic. For whatever reason, I suppressed those inner most volcanoes of emotions from erupting. Teary-eyed, I swallowed continually while staring at a vast nothingness to maintain my composure. It served me well during the daytime but a soggy pillow bore witness to my nighttime difficulties. Those mind torturing engines refused to grant me an easy road to a restful sleep as a multitude of episodes my son and I shared replayed in my mind, over and over again. Nights didn't provide any comfort in the form of dreams, just a battering ram of questions and guilt pounding my head well into the morning hours. The rising sun freed me from my nightly prison, but progressing through the day lacking proper sleep became another gauntlet needing to be faced.

Coping with a major loss is never easy and everyone's road to inner acceptance and peace winds differently. Some people never complete the journey. There often comes a time when many turn their moistened eyes towards God in hopes of receiving the comfort society and friends are unable to provide. Comfort is derived from the belief our deceased loved one is happy and well in the embrace of the Divine. Loss then becomes a continuing journey of letting go. While many will never complete the journey, others not only complete it but grow emotionally and psychologically as well. My journey is a slow one as I still have an occasional relapse that seems to come out of nowhere. I surmise my passage will end when I will also experience the loving Light and embrace my son again.

Peace of mind, when it came, was, however, only temporary. Unannounced a billboard, a song, a face or a gentle, kissing breeze reaches into my inner depth where, like a dormant cicada, emotions suddenly erupt like a volcano. Haunting memories never seem to go away and as long as they linger, a certain emotional vulnerability remains, eternally connected to a water well deep within the psyche. Prayers for comfort and peace are no match for internal feelings constantly on the brink of eruption. My shoulders could never feel the comforting hand of Jesus the Christ as my heart continued its arrhythmic pounding of misery.

As a parent, it is unfathomable that your child should leave this earthly plane before you do. As a brother, it pains knowing your life-long partner is gone, leaving an unimaginable void. As a young daughter, the shock of suddenly losing a major supporting figure in life is crushingly overwhelming and demoralizing. While each individual handles loss in their own way, coping is something we must all do for life marches forward, stopping for no one or no thing.

There was a time when Johnny invited me to New York and photograph a job he was working on in the Rockaways after Hurricane Sandy decimated the area. He was euphorically energized and had visions of growing his electrical business to unlimited heights. It was in the middle of the night when he jostled me awake. "Call 911, I think I'm having a heart attack!" I jumped out of bed, as his girlfriend Kyley had already called for help. Sitting on the floor, waiting for the ambulance to arrive, he looked straight into my eyes and declared, "Promise me, you'll take care of my girls!"

Taken aback, I replied, "Fuck you! You take care of your girls. You're not going anywhere!"

Was it a precursor for what was to happen? I don't know, but the panic attack he suffered that night ignited a reminder as to how fragile life can be. His concern was always his girls who provided the meaning and love he was craving, while also providing a much-needed escape from life's pressures, which were consuming him. With Emma and Kylie he dropped his austere facade and became a light-hearted, fun-loving elf everyone admired. Around his girls, he was Johnny B!

Today, however, things are dramatically different, as life has steered my ship in a direction I was ill prepared for. It was one thing arguing with him, it's quite another losing him forever. Regardless how much we argued, there was always the probability that, at some point in time, we would talk and smooth things out. While I can direct my feelings and thoughts heavenward, I will never again feel the thrill of his hugs or a kiss on the lips. This is a memory I will always have of him, and a pain that will never leave. How God fit into this most tragic moment, I do not know and will probably never understand. I was unable to read the tea leaves life presented me and for that I will forever mourn.

Chapter - 3

Look Out God Here I Come

"Your life is like a book:
A book of intrigue, a book of adventure, a book of love, a book of joy,
a book of sadness.
Not only are you its reader,
you are also its author."

—Spirit

I felt my body rocking back and forth, but not sure why. In the distance I could hear a voice, but couldn't make out what was being said or who was calling me. Slowly it came closer as the shaking increased. Uneasiness was beginning to turn into fear.

"Get up! You have to get up it's almost noon." The message was repeated several times.

"What's going on?"

"Get up! I'm not going to let you sleep the day away. Let's go! You need to get outside, go for a walk."

Thank goodness the shaking had stopped. "OK, OK, relax, I'm getting up!"

"I want you to get out of the house today, get some fresh air," Jannette instructed. A calming peace began to return as I realized it was my wife encouraging me to leave my self-imposed confinement. Time was slowly becoming my enemy as she recognized the early signs of depression.

Within a half hour I found myself walking along the Cherry Creek Trail. There weren't too many bicycle riders today. I looked around at the blooming wild flowers and listened to the songs of the local finches. My mind discarded all of its clutter as I breathed deeply basking in nature's healing energy. It was the perfect remedy to slowly evaporate the mental chains of sadness.

I was in a malaise! Life's importance had somehow slipped away from me. What was the meaning of life anyway when it could be so abruptly interrupted and cut short? Interestingly enough, it's not the physical toil imposing undue strain on the body, as the body is quite resilient when it comes to physical stress. No, it's the psychological trauma, which drains the body's ability to survive and cope more than anything physical. Self-inflicted mental torture can last a lifetime and no one can rescue you from this self- imposed prison. Although they're not made of iron, these bars are much stronger and more intimidating. But here on the trail, the song of birds, smell of flowers and kiss of the soft breeze reenergized me. A feeling of rebirth began to rejuvenate my soul. Jannette's love and caring would, I was sure, see me through this difficult time.

Forgetting and letting go are, however, two different things. While I could never forget, it was imperative to let go. Nothing can prepare you for losing a child. Regardless of the relationship, it hurts. Its pain is magnified when the relationship is already strained and you can never recapture the good times or, worse yet, repair the bad ones. It comes out of nowhere, this rush of pain driven tears, not caring where you are or whom you're with. All you can do is say, "Excuse me, I'll be right back." Your sudden leaving and blood shot eyes when you return cannot mask your internal mayhem. Previous suppression of those feelings only delays the inevitable mental eruption, and, somehow magnifies their intensity.

It was my brother-in-law, John, who had given me the best advice, "It's OK to grieve the loss, but it's not OK to blame yourself." Somehow I needed to free myself from this prison of blame and accept the loss. The choice to leave this world lay with my son, not with me. Not being able to say goodbye or fix a fractured relationship continued to haunt me for months, as guilt became my cross to bear. But I knew Jannette was right, getting out was the first step to recovery.

After months of staring into outer space, barely aware of those around me, I somehow came to the conclusion that God was at fault. I remembered my mom refusing to speak of the war years during my childhood. Finally, I understood her anguish. Why, God? There cannot be any logical reason why my son came to this drastic conclusion he had to terminate his time on earth. I could not understand it then, and I cannot understand it today. Why God?

Once the well of tears had run dry, I began to look for a culprit. Who could influence my son to such a degree? Who had that much power? Looking around at family and friends I could identify several people who maintained a high level of influence, but no one who could drive him over the edge. It had to be the same, uncaring God my mother sent countless prayers to many years ago. So, who was this God? I had to find out!

Some memories come floating forward more readily than others, but they all appeared to have the same effects, physical and psychological break down. Tears flowed more easily these days as I let go of my internal stoicism and embraced the world of pain and regret more readily. But forgiving God for my misery and, more importantly, taking my son from me was quite another matter. It now became important for me to find out who this all-powerful deity was and what purpose he served. I believe the remnants and aftermath of the war had left my mother embracing the world of agnosticism. If I were to follow her path, I would at least do my due diligence to find out who God was, if he existed at all and how I fit into his domain. For some reason I could not embrace the belief my existence here was purely arbitrary and without meaning. "Look out God, here I come!" The scream went unheard by the trees and nearby birds but it was ear splitting to me. I had thrown down the gauntlet. I felt better.

The following morning, I slowly dressed, putting on a pair of comfortable shorts and a short sleeved, loose fitting blue crew neck.

Coming downstairs I saw Jannette sitting in the living room chair, welcoming my decision to join the rest of the world.

"I'm going to take a walk along the trail." She nodded and went back to reading her morning affirmations from the Science of Mind Magazine.

After a quick bowl of Rice Krispies and my usual dose of morning vitamins, I put on my sneakers and headed out the door. "Have fun," she called out as the door was closing behind me.

"Will do." I began walking towards the trailhead at the end of the cul-de-sac as my mind was already ramping up random thoughts, which had very little significance at this moment or time. They just kept coming until this avalanche of ideas threatened to suck me into its whirlpool of "how come" and "what ifs," questions which had been asked countless times but which I was unable to answer. As happened often, I sought refuge in the distant past. The years of my youth and adolescence were far enough removed from my internal guilt I could not shake. I welcomed the change and embraced the replay of my younger years. My search for God would begin here.

Somewhere, somehow along the line, I became indoctrinated into believing in a judgmental god whose wrath and jealousy remained with me throughout much of my lifetime. Churches, as my grandfather undoubtedly believed, tend to impede people's advancement through their dogma by ensnaring individuals in doctrines more intent on serving the church body. Teaching the need for forgiveness, the importance of holy sacraments, the infallibility of the church hierarchy, tithing and the wrath of God, only serves to imprison people in a belief system from which there is little hope of escape. After all, the church had the inside track as the individual's intermediary by paving the way to God's forgiveness and righteousness. Ingrained principles imbedded into the psyche at a young age are difficult to let go of even as one matures.

With this upbringing, I began religious studies at Bethany Lutheran Church when I was in junior high school. What prompted my parents to enroll me in church and to learn about the dogma of God was well beyond my understanding. God was rarely invited to our table. However, once a week it allowed me to leave school early and that was always a good thing.

It was during my confirmation classes when I heard about a new Lutheran high school opening for the 1960 school year. After taking an initial entrance exam, I was accepted to attend Martin Luther High School in Woodside, New York. Confirmation enabled me to partake in the Holy Communion Sacrament, which served to strengthen my belief in a forgiving God, one who was somewhere out there and needed to be acknowledged and respected. Prayer became the recommended communication system whenever it became necessary to contact God for need or forgiveness. God became this external, all-powerful, all-knowing and ever-present being from whom there was no escape. Beliefs from my childhood years were solidified and enhanced; it was through required church participation, support and embracing the prevailing dogma that people would be saved from eternal damnation. I drank the Kool-Aid! The church, it seemed, had the inside track to God and his goodness. My youthful fear of God and the church were somewhat alleviated as I came to understand God's message of infinite love and eternal life. Suddenly ministers became teachers, helping me to understand the message of God, and not the fearful administrators of His judgment, as I had believed. Indoctrination into the Christian faith was well on its way with little or no resistance from me.

As I grew, I began to understand the church was instrumental in showing me, beyond a shadow of a doubt, a God who is loving and kind and wants us all to succeed and have the very best life has to offer. Unfortunately, all too often life and societal expectancies cloud the path to spiritual introspection while illuminating the road to financial and personal success. All too often life and societal expectancies lead us towards a path of selfishness and materialism. I became torn between the paths of enlightenment and worldly success. I chose the more immediate need, ignoring one basic tenet, "With God all things are possible." (Matthew 19:26)

I had reached Cherry Creek, a little stream about 200 yards from my home. There was an area with a six-foot drop acting as a mini waterfall surrounded by large rocks offering a secluded area with ample privacy from the main path to minimize any intrusion. I sat down and closed my eyes listening to the rush of water and the whispering of leaves from the slight breeze. Had I a pillow I would have undoubtedly fallen asleep.

It was my sister-in-law Ruth who first opened the gateway to spirituality with her belief in meditation, past life regression, reincarnation and Reiki. While the message resonated within me, its principles were a bit more difficult to fathom and put into practice. My mind, however, had been made aware that God may be different than I had first imagined. For me, the door for change had been opened.

As I continued my mental childhood journey another favorite Bible passage emerged onto the screen of my mind, "The Kingdom of God is within you" (Luke 17:21). This quote was followed by, "Seek the kingdom of God above all else, and He will give you everything you need" (Luke 12:31). Marianne Williamson followed with, "We were born to manifest the glory of God that is within us." After reading and studying these and other similar writings, I began to understand our dichotomy of God and began to shift my thinking from a God with-out to a God with-in. Not only did this make much more sense to me, but it now put me in a place where Divine Spirit was more easily accessible and much less intimidating. Had God taken up my challenge? Was this his response? I took out my cell phone and began to do a Google search on who and what God was and ran into several quotes that made some sense to me. First, Swami Vivekananda summed it up well when he stated, "All that is real in me is God...Thus by knowing God, we find that the kingdom of heaven is within us." Then I found a Muhammad Ali quote where he proudly proclaimed:

"We all have the same God, we just serve him differently. Rivers, lakes, ponds, streams, oceans all have different names, but they all contain water. So do religions have different names, and they all contain truth, expressed in different ways, forms and times. It doesn't matter whether you're a Muslim, a Christian, or a Jew. When you believe in God, you should believe that all people are part of one family. If you love God, you can't love only some of his children."

Then there was T.B. Joshua who takes Muhammad Ali's lesson a bit deeper and proclaims a more intimate relationship between God and mankind.

"There is no one ugly, deep, dark, powerful or evil enough to stop God from loving you. Nothing anyone can ever do to you can sever your connection to God. Nothing you could ever do can dam the unstoppable love of God for you. His love for you is undeniable, unrelenting and unconditional. You may ignore God, ridicule Him and reject Him but His love for you will remain constant and unchanging...When the Spirit of God comes into us, He wants to be Himself in us. He wants His energy to be poured through us. He wants His wisdom to be deposited in our hearts. He wants His instinct and nature to be evident and obvious in you. He wants us to see what He is looking at, to feel what He feels, to know what He knows, to work with His projects, see life the way He sees it, get His ideas and know His opinion about yourself and others...Jesus wants to express Himself and carry out His mission of love to others through you."

These insights certainly were more informative than the standard Christian tenets I had been taught throughout my lifetime. But how does this work? Stating concepts without revealing how it actually works was, for me, counterproductive. So God was inside me. So what? What exactly did it mean and how do I contact Him and, more importantly, how does He respond to me? After all, I could attest to countless pleading prayers aimed at the betterment of life that went unheeded. As for me, prayers only entered my life when a dire emergency arose. I came to understand prayers professed in church were more rote than meaningful expressions from the heart.

I thought about my grandfather's message that one doesn't have to go to church to believe in God was never intended to proclaim a dogma or spiritual belief in a higher being. It did, nevertheless, expound on his belief the church body was more concerned with self-advancement rather than growing people's spiritual awareness. For him, the church was a model of opulence supported by people with meager earnings and limited means. Alexander Mahns had the insight to know God was someone who did not require to be worshipped from the altar of a church sanctuary, but God was receptive to all men regardless of their church affiliation. As a Communist his beliefs were presumably influenced by Karl Marx who stated, "The first requisite for the happiness of the people is the abolition of religion." It is, therefore, little wonder that he had slight regard for organized religion or its system of beliefs. My grandfather's influence ultimately filtered to my mother and, to some extent, to me. Until my teens, God remained an individual, an overseer who watched and cared for his flock, much like a shepherd. Whatever I didn't fully understand was easily dismissed as life's necessities would never diminish and were never resolved as a result of any message coming from the pulpit.

After several hikes to my private waterfall, meditation on my favorite rock became something I looked forward to; internal reflection was still something I didn't fully understand. While it gave me some spiritual insights, I never quite understood how to make it work for me or what its greater intentions were. My subjective mind helped me to journey to scenic and restful places to help me clear any physical tensions remaining from hectic and stressful days. Meditation certainly helped me sleep better and, on occasion, was a means to fall asleep.

Things began to change a bit when I dared to ask a question during one of my meditations, "Who am I?"

It did not take long for the internal reply to formulate in my consciousness. "You are what I am. I am love, you are love; I am peace, you are peace; I am the great creator, you are the great creator.

Whatever I do, you do and I am with you always. I experience life through you." This unexpected response, while welcome, left me with more questions. How could this be? At the moment the only love I felt was for my family; while peace or calmness was achieved through meditation, it would be gone again tomorrow as a new day presented itself; and what I created came about through hard work and sacrifice. The rest of the message seemed like pure hogwash or, at the very least, incomprehensible. I understood the words but couldn't see what they were telling me. Had some of these principles been presented on Sunday mornings, I may not have rejected them as readily. How could I possibly be on the same level with a being who required my regular contrition while struggling through daily issues of survival? Give me a sign! Answer some prayers!

Receiving a response during meditation, regardless of its reliability, did, however, give me the wherewithal to continue meditating. Messages, however, infrequent, were more strategic in nature and, with limited time and ability I rarely found the opportunity to delve deeply into them. In addition, they seemed to be the same message presented over and over again in different words. Either I didn't understand or my mind was somehow messing with me. Regardless, real, tangible advice was never forthcoming or seemed to be lost in a quagmire of misunderstood or irrelevant messages. Reasoning was not a meditative strong suit as it seemingly ignored the fruits of Descartes and other great philosophers.

Meditative messages, however, did cause me to delve deeper into the founders of religion and their teachings. Jesus, Buddha, Mohammad and others were the great teachers attempting to point us in the right direction. Churches built around their teachings were, I began to realize, meant to enlighten people, not enslave them in principles and sacraments. For many, the church body provides guidance and ideals, which help with spiritual understanding and growth. Anyone who chooses to join a church is well on his/her way to divine insight and the understanding of a higher power we call God, and this is always a good thing. The road to enlightenment is never straight or easy, but it is a path we all hope to follow one day. After all, it is important to know that all roads ultimately lead to God. As Walter Starcke stated in his book *The Third Appearance*:

"God is a state of consciousness that can be experienced anywhere, not something that can be found in a particular place. Our own higher consciousness is our church or synagogue, and it goes everywhere we go. Whenever we feel the presence of higher consciousness while sharing with others we are in church. There are places where we more easily sense an all-inclusive oneness than in other locations - most often in nature or while listening to inspiring music - and those places are our church."

I began to wonder about those who reject the spiritual nature or existence of God and profess the universe and our lives as nothing more than a link in the great evolutionary chain of events. What about those who believe we are all here for a brief moment in time and once our lifetime ends we return to the dust from whence we came? Do those beliefs exempt us from believing in, or being accountable, to any external forces except those created by civilized beings to create some law and order in this vast, diverse civilization?

To me, it appears such believers would be more focused on day-to-day events and needs necessary to augment and enhance the means required to meet daily obligations and issues life brings their way. However, even daily survival requires prioritizing necessities and relationships, which often lead to roads of success or failure. Personal values become, therefore, the cumulative focus of internal and external means of survival. I could visualize a common definition of god as an image, person or thing who is worshipped, honored or believed to be all-powerful. Hence, god doesn't have to be spiritual or material, eternal or temporal, enlightened or intolerant, god can be anything or anyone one deems to be important or necessary for success. God, therefore, can be the need for wealth, power or notoriety. God, therefore, can take the shape of tangible possessions such as mansions or money, or intangible influences such as power or authority.

After some research, I found these non-spiritual advocates often adhere to a naturalistic philosophy maintaining nature encompasses all that exists and operates according to the principles of physics and natural laws. In their world the supernatural does not exist. In the words of Carl Sagan, "The Cosmos is all that is or ever was or ever will be." While this is certainly a very brief synopsis of naturalism, it, nevertheless, leads to a very interesting dichotomy; is there a spiritual domain or, more importantly, does God exist?

Articles, papers, books and ad-nauseam discussions throughout the ages, have been documented for and against the arguments for the existence of God. I certainly did not intend to go through that rabbit hole for it would be far too overwhelming for me to decipher and tackle such a vast and controversial subject. God, as I began to understand, appears to hold a very personal and intrinsic ideal for each individual and is, therefore, subject to many interpretations.

Philosophers who argued for the existence of God can be traced back to Plato and Aristotle. They also include St. Anselm, Thomas Aquinas, John Calvin and Rene Descartes, whose, "I think, therefore I am," at least proves my existence and I am eternally grateful to him for that. Those who oppose the existence of God include Friedrich Nietzsche, Bertrand Russell, Stephen Hawking and Carl Sagan. Both sides include some of the greatest philosophers to ever walk this planet, yet nowhere did I find the secret for putting these concepts in motion and incorporating them in day-to-day living.

Personal history has fortified my belief in the existence of a higher power, someone or something that has existed and will continue to exist eternally. Can I prove it beyond a shadow of a doubt, probably not? Reflections on my meditative rock began to slowly erode my internal iron bars of doubt and shortsightedness. But do I have an internal, intangible connection to a consciousness that helps me to react instinctively to events or situations, a consciousness making me aware of what is inherently right or wrong, good or evil, a consciousness that does not follow the laws of physics or is something that cannot be scientifically verified or analyzed? I began to formulate a new construct, we are all conscious beings driven by our thoughts and desires; we innately know the difference between love and hate, likes and dislikes; we understand empathy and heartlessness; we feel the difference between brotherhood and separation. These are all qualities, which go beyond the animalistic needs of self-preservation; they are qualities and behavioral traits of a higher order. Kudos! It seemed like I had finally moved from my longstanding understanding of God and began to reach out to the intangible world of spiritual consciousness.

Geologically speaking, we are here on this planet but for an instant. With an approximate lifespan of approximately seventy years, our impact on this world, for the most part, is minimal and insignificant. So what then is the purpose for our brief visit to this world? I have problems believing that somehow, out of this vast ocean of evolution, we, as a species, emerged to grow a mighty civilization only to have it evaporate in a universe filled with chaos and uncertainty. It seemed to me, the seventy or so years I will spend here are not inconsequential; they provide a learning opportunity given to me by a Higher Power to help me evolve into the very best conscious being possible. Since this connection is not physical, it can never be validated scientifically, but it exists, nevertheless, intrinsically embedded into my ability to think, understand and reason. I do not have to go to church to believe in God, all I need to do is to look inward and listen to those instinctive messages, which continue to proclaim my connection to an Almighty God. As Walter Starcke states, "Great temples or cathedrals have been built more for the purpose of intimidating people and encouraging them to accept the authority of the establishment than to honor God." There are no intermediaries required for anyone to know God, "God is divine mind. We can't change it, but we can have access to it."

All these philosophical ideals surrounding God and who He is are difficult enough to understand without any deep personal involvement. Spirit, it has been noted, often works in mysterious and strange ways. Heavenly messages are often subtle and obscure but, occasionally, they come out of nowhere with the smashing impact of a sledgehammer. While I was moving deeper into spiritual understanding the reasons for the loss of my son continued to escape me. My big dilemma began to surface from within, "How does this all work?" Words are often persuasive but they need to be properly digested to elicit any meaningful response. My challenge to God had become clear: I hear your words; show me how to follow your path!

Chapter - 4

The Academy

"Expand your mind. Enrich your life."
—Spirit

Throughout my life, God had been a second-class citizen. Losing my son would, however, open the doorway to the possibility of a caring Deity and the existence of an afterlife. Somehow, I still needed the assurance Johnny was safe and unharmed. His untimely death spurred me on to search for a deeper understanding of God. While my basic concepts of God lay in the foundation of Christian doctrines, specifically in the Protestant branch founded by Martin Luther, those beliefs were now being revisited.

The Bible I learned was to be taken literally and contrition for one's sins necessary to gain access to everlasting glory. Blindly I accepted the beliefs in original sin and its cleansing Sacrament of Baptism; I felt the need to partake in Holy Communion as a means of receiving forgiveness; and I understood the Ten Commandments to be the roadmap leading to a better life here on earth and in the afterlife. Yes, I believed in an afterlife and being confronted with the possibility of spending it in the eternal fires of hell kept me from totally drifting away from my religious roots. Better to be safe than sorry. Heaven also offered a personal assurance in knowing my dear son did not just return to dust.

My path through life was certainly not straight and narrow; it included almost every turn and misstep imaginable. Life, as it does so often, always seems to get in the way. There was a career to pursue, children to raise and a family to feed. Who had time to sit and decipher the meaning of God and all the religious teaching demanding my supplication? It would take a failed marriage and the pressures of fighting a divorce while raising four teenagers to finally lead me to the self-introspection necessary to decipher the meaning of life while establishing its priorities. Somehow I came to the conclusion it was not pleasing those around me but building a solid personal foundation that would lead me out of the doldrums of life. Unfortunately it took the loss of my youngest son for this life changing revelation to manifest itself.

It is no surprise, therefore, I was drawn to a website for The Academy for Lifelong Learning offering stimulating intellectual and social learning opportunities for mature adults in a classroom environment. Of the many courses offered, one, in particular, jumped out at me. "All Things God" sounded interestingly ambiguous and its syllabus was intriguing to say the least. The course included, among others, lessons on consciousness, the creative process, the God dichotomy and the I Am.

Why was my internal intuitive mechanism vibrating as I read the synopsis? I am not a religious scholar, nor am I a minister advocating the message of a belief system, nor am I a zealot caught up in the dogmas of any particular creed, nor was I a member of a household whose activities were bound by the politics of any religion. My background in religion or spirituality, however you would describe it, was much more unassuming. With my new tendency to question things and to occasionally read books whose central messages reside in the depths of philosophical reasoning often created a whirlwind of questions that, for the large part, became central to my research and re-evaluation of my belief system.

Through the years, I have come to believe in God or in some Higher Power who is central to our existence and the universe, as we know it; while I don't quite understand them, I believe in its omnipotence, omniscience and omnipresence. Most importantly, I believe in God's goodness, empathy and compassion; attributes most religions or beliefs identify as love and forgiveness. What this Higher Power is, or where It resides, or how we are connected to It, has been debated for ages. In a world where scientific proof is required to silence the skeptics, God is not a tangible being. Rather He exists, I've been told, in our innate consciousness refusing to be silenced and continuing to ask questions that spur me on to seek answers.

Sensing an ability to ask questions, which invariably arose while reading books, increased the class' appeal. Malachi, with no last name, was the instructor. While he didn't have a lengthy list of acronyms to his name, his name does, however, appear in the Bible and is simply translated from Hebrew as "my messenger." Was this a moment of synchronicity as described in the *Celestine Prophesy*? There was only one way to find out. Filling out the appropriate form and verifying the site's encryption, I entered my credit card information. This class may not provide the answers to my questions, I thought, but at least it offered a platform where I could ask them. God and spirituality were about to become more clearly defined for me and hopefully in a receptive way.

Without hesitating, I signed up for the class hoping to expand my spiritual horizons and, although unlikely, finally understanding what God is all about. Religions and their strict ideologies were, I felt, too narrow in scope in their dogma and failed to fully define the God concept. Believing in a deity requiring one's belief in ancient doctrines established by a dominating church intent on subjugating the masses did not resonate with me. Certainly the life of Jesus was interesting and insightful, but his life was filled with inherent possibilities for all of us. "With God all things are possible," was one of the biblical passages I held dear. It says nothing about a necessary belief system based on forgiveness of sins in order to gain His favor.

My challenge to God was becoming clearer as old values and beliefs were being seriously questioned and I wasn't sure where this road would lead or whether I would find the answers I was looking for. What made this even more obscure, I wasn't entirely sure what questions to ask. Learning, I have found, especially when it comes to religion and spirituality, is a matter of preference and feeling of comfort. Understanding my search for spiritual clarity could possibly lead me in many different directions, I formulated a plan to accept only those principles, which resonated within me. Before accepting any philosophy concerning any deity, I would need to feel comfortable with its doctrine. With this basic guideline I forged forward to find the meaning of God. For a brief second I pondered, "Was this my idea or was this God's way of accepting my challenge?" It didn't matter. It was my comfort level and understanding at risk, not God's.

"I signed up for a class at The Academy for Lifelong Learning," I yelled to Jannette, who was somewhere in the house.

A Science of Mind Practitioner, Jannette understood my dilemma and helped me to more clearly understand the spiritual side of things. Through the years, her attempt to clarify the difference between religion and spirituality fell largely on deaf ears. It seemed the loss of my son created an internal curiosity to understand the connection between my tangible world and the spiritual. The time had come for me to finally recognize the consequences of my earlier decisions and to, at least, give God a chance. It was through her insight I recognized that religion and spirituality are quite different and synergistically opposed. An avid reader, she introduced me to books aimed at helping me gain a clearer perspective in spirituality by exploring insight and possibilities without limitations. Having grown up with a perception of limitations and an ideology of work ethic being paramount, these new concepts took hold quickly in a mind ripe for knowledge.

Her reply came quickly, "What is that?"

"It's an adult learning place here in Denver. They cater to adults who are interested in further learning."

I must have piqued her interest as I heard her coming down the stairs, "What are you planning on taking?"

"A course called 'All Things God.'"

"Sounds very interesting. What are you looking to get out of it?"

"Not sure, it just hit me as something that could be interesting. Science of Mind and typical religion are so far apart. Maybe this will explain it all a bit better."

"Then do it. I'm all for anything that helps people grow and understand the spiritual nature of things. "

"I already signed up."

"Good, when do you start?"

"In a little over a month."

"Hope you find what you're looking for," she yelled as she scurried back upstairs, "I think it will be good for you."

While familiar with the basic Science of Mind principles, I was looking for more. Simple superficial teachings about God's role in our lives didn't silence the questions continually rising within my psyche. There had to be so much more to this God whose teachings and belief system were so instrumental in today's society. How did this Divine Being become a central focus in our lives? If He were this entity embracing love and forgiveness why would He allow all these atrocities and biases to exist in this world? Hopefully this Malachi person had the insight into my personal self to calm the tsunami of questions and doubts so prevalent within my soul. Anyone, I thought, who had the courage to tackle such a controversial subject must have some special insights. Internally I felt assured my questions would be answered and doubts erased. Either God would be dismissed as a folly or I would gain the inner strength required to embrace Him unconditionally.

As evening brought a more calming influence to my demeanor, I decided to meditate. After several deep breaths my body fell into a deep, relaxing state. I found myself on a ledge near a mountaintop, dressed in Native American attire with a lone tree beside me. Overlooking a deep chasm, I was subliminally messaged to climb the tree either upward or downward depending on what I was searching for.

I climbed up through the branches and found myself in a peaceful, white environment with a marble bench and a high-steeple building in the distance. I sat on the bench, immersed in the serenity and simplicity around me. It didn't take long as a figure in a white robe approached me and sat next to me on the bench. "I am Teacher," I could hear him say telepathically, "what brings you here?"

"I am at a crossroads. I need to know if my son is well and how I can better understand spirituality and apply it to my day-to-day living."

"Johnny is well, as we all are in the realm of the Divine. Living a spiritual life is easy; all you need do is to choose to do it. The hard part is to not allow all your earthly distractions to get in the way."

"How do I do that?"

"It takes patience and conviction. It's not as simple as taking off one coat and putting on another. You need to make the change internally. Let your intuition dictate your life, not the external forces that lead you astray."

"How do I do that?"

"Start by taking the class. It will help lay the foundation necessary for understanding what spirituality actually is. From there you will come to know who you really are."

I left the Teacher with a calm and tranquil mind; assured attending the Academy's class would provide some, if not all, the answers I was looking for. I slept comfortably that night.

Chapter - 5

Malachi

"Conscious awareness is enhanced with the embodiment of Spirit."
—Spirit

"God is...what?" I thought.

Traveling north along Interstate 25, I found myself in the throes of Denver's morning rush hour. While nothing compared to the Long Island Expressway, traffic had been steadily getting worse as more people relocated to this state of scenic beauty and filled with career opportunities. Fortunately I didn't have to travel all the way to Denver and exited on Hampden Avenue just past the Denver Tech Center. After a quick left on Monaco the Calvary Baptist Church stood before me on the right side of the street. Fortunately I had arrived early enough where parking was not yet an issue.

Calvary Baptist did not look like a church when I first entered, but more like a school. After a large foyer area there were hallways leading to numerous classrooms. The main worship area, hidden behind closed doors, looked like a good-sized movie theater with a large crucifix and a tapestry adorning the back of the altar area. Large ranks of silver pipes dominated either side of the altar area. A sizeable cafeteria, set up with almost 20 tables for a popular bridge class acted as a buffer between the foyer and classrooms.

A smiling lady with glasses sitting at the tip of her nose, sitting behind the information desk, directed me to the classrooms in the rear. A sign "All Things God" welcomed me as I entered classroom three. An older man deeply immersed in a book was standing before a whiteboard to my left and began writing "I AM..." Gauging by his appearance, he was well on in years. It wasn't just the white hair and beard, but the lines of wisdom etched into his face, which made the greatest impression on me. He was probably close to six feet tall if his slight hunch ever straightened out. Despite his small potbelly, he still maintained a sense of dignity reminiscent of someone who deserved to be treated with respect and whose words were meaningful and filled with purpose. If he weren't the teacher of a class in Denver, I would not be surprised if he were one of the ancient mystics who served to enlighten mankind.

He didn't wear the long, flowing saffron robe of the sages but rather jeans and a wrinkled plaid shirt more appropriate for this part of the western United States. His opened-toed sandals were probably the only attire somewhat out of place, and his colorful walking stick, hanging on a chair, reminded me more of a mini totem pole than an actual cane.

But what was most interesting was his demeanor. Here was a man whose aura, I'm sure, reflected the color of enlightenment. In spite of his wrinkled face, his features radiated truth and wisdom, honesty and joy and love and compassion. Before me stood a man whose insight into the reality of things, I was sure, was deep and profound; and he had yet to utter a word.

"Hi," I said entering the room and breaking his thought pattern, "is this the 'All Things God' class?"

"Yes, welcome, I'm Malachi. Please have a seat."

The tables and chairs were organized in a horseshoe pattern and I chose the middle chair on the right side. "I'm Hans Benes," I replied as I laid out my notebook on the table. Just then an elderly lady entered the classroom with a cursory hello and sat opposite me. Before too long, five students, all at or approaching retirement age, had taken their seats and eagerly awaited the start of the class.

"I see we're all here," Malachi began, "before we begin, why don't we all introduce ourselves by completing the 'I AM...' statement on the board and telling everyone why you're here. Let's begin with this young lady here."

"I AM Mary," the blonde-haired lady replied, "and I'm here to get a deeper understanding of who or what God truly is."

"Good, I hope you will find an answer to your questions," Malachi responded, "next."

"I AM Paul," the man next to Mary replied. His demeanor was one of an educated person who seemed very assured of himself and, I was sure, was a ranking manager during his professional years. "I'm here to see what God looks like outside of the religious norm."

"Interesting," replied Malachi, "I'm not sure He looks any different regardless of where He is. But I'm hopeful that you might have a better understanding of who He is by the time this class is over. How about you, young lady?"

"I AM Joanne and I'm here to better understand how God can impact my life in a more structured and meaningful way."

Malachi smiled softly, "Don't we all want our lives to be more impactful and meaningful. Including God in one's life can certainly make a huge difference. And you, young lady?"

The elderly lady who had entered behind me smiled and stated simply, "I AM Sarah and I'm just here to learn."

"Great, Sarah," Malachi replied jubilantly, "isn't that something we all can do throughout our lifetime? As long as you keep an open mind, I'm sure you'll learn quite a bit. And you, sir?"

"I AM Hans and I'm here to find out who I really am," I replied.

Malachi hesitated a bit as his eyes rolled skyward before replying, almost as though he was searching for the answer to be etched deep within the ceiling. "You have come to the right place! We all think we know who we are, but the reality of things might surprise us all. Hopefully, by the end of this course we'll all have a clearer understanding of who we are. And I'm Malachi. I'm no religious scholar just a normal person with some spiritual insight to share."

He picked up some handouts from his desk and continued, "Let me hand out a few pages of information about what we'll cover in this class and I also invite you to visit my shop in Evergreen if you've a mind to travel up that way. So let's start," he began as he erased the 'I AM...' from the whiteboard, replacing it with, "Cogito, ergo sum."

"I think, therefore I am?" it was more of a question than a statement from Paul.

"Correct! Since this first class is about consciousness, does anyone want to venture and take a guess whether thinking makes one conscious?"

"Yes," Paul answered without hesitation, "by thinking we exercise the power of our mind which spurs our consciousness."

"Interesting," came Malachi's response, "anyone else?" No one dared to raise their hand, quite possibly for fear of being wrong. Had Paul's eagerness stepped into some unseen quicksand? "What is consciousness, does anyone want to take a guess?"

"An awareness of oneself?" I offered, more as a question than a statement of fact.

Malachi smiled at me, "That's about as close as we can understand. For anyone to think, they would have to be conscious first. You can't think without being aware. So, before the material universe began roughly 13 billion years ago, consciousness existed. That universal consciousness was, as best as we humans can understand, God. There are two basic theories about the creation of man: one is presented in the Bible where God created Adam and Eve, while the other is the big bang, which physicists claim began the ultimate cycle of evolution culminating with our existence here on earth. While no one knows for sure how we got here does it really make any difference?" Malachi looked around at five perplexed faces all trying their best to avoid his eyes, hoping he wouldn't call on them.

"No?" I offered.

"Why?" came his quick reply.

"It was a 50-50 shot," I replied shrugging my shoulders, "I just figured that regardless of how we got here, God would have had something to do with it."

"I can't argue with that reasoning. But the important point I'm trying to make is regardless how we came to be, Universal Consciousness was instrumental in our creation. Going a bit further, if we owe our existence to Universal Consciousness, does it not stand to reason God would have instilled consciousness within his created beings? Without consciousness all His creations would be pretty pictures or statues without life or meaning. And if we are to believe the big bang theory, did it not come from a point of singularity, or oneness? If that Oneness was conscious of itself, did its consciousness not remain within the remnants of this event?"

"Are you saying everything has consciousness?" Joanne interrupted. "Do you have children, Joanne?"

"Yes."

"And, assuming they're conscious, where did they get their consciousness from?" Joanne laughed, "Sometimes I wonder about that, but they got it from me."

"So can we not also surmise we received our consciousness from our creator, and, as a result, we are connected consciously to Him?" Malachi looked around the class where five people seemed to be deeply immersed in thought. Critical thinking, I'm sure he reasoned, was always a good thing. "What is important to understand here is our connection to God; everything and everyone we see or come in contact with has its root beginning in the Universal Consciousness and, as such, we are all connected to God. When you come down to it, this entire universe is truly 'All Things God.' Everything, including animals, plants, rocks and the seas, had its beginning from the Universal Consciousness and is, therefore, bound by the same science we are bound by, such as gravity and electromagnetism. Their fundamental makeup includes electrons, neutrons and protons prevalent in all things in our universe. The Universal Whole embodies everything we know and see. Nothing can exist outside of it. A rock might not be able to think, but the God Consciousness, which created it is inherent in its makeup. How else can our spiritual scholars declare the omnipresence of God? The big difference is the rock is not aware of itself because it doesn't have the capacity to think. The sixteenth century Italian philosopher Francesco Patrizi coined the phrase Panpsychism, which is the view all things have a mind or a mind-like quality and the term derives its meaning from the two Greek words pan (all) and psyche (soul or mind)."

"So, if I'm understanding this correctly, everything is embodied with the God particles, but it's the ability to think that sets us apart?" Sarah asked in a measured voice, making sure each word was appropriately stated.

Malachi smiled, "You're starting to get the idea. God is everywhere. It was no accident that I called this class 'All Things God.' Wherever you see material things or wherever consciousness resides, there you will find God."

Malachi certainly had me thinking. His brief reference to omnipresence resurrected an internal confusion about how anyone or anything could be everywhere at once. Add to it omniscience and omnipotence and you have a being who surpasses all understanding. I don't think Descartes, as he tried to understand his own existence, ever took his philosophical reasoning so deep. The old man had, whether inadvertently or not, awakened my thirst for the understanding of things I, unfortunately, had often taken for granted. Through the course of too many years I had become decisively lacking in my ability to think critically. Maybe it wasn't ability but desire, as my willing acceptance of messages from "those in the know" became an easy way out, requiring little or no introspection. Years of personal growth lay by the wayside as I embraced the beating drum of societal norms and directives.

"Let's lighten things up a bit, shall we?" Malachi continued, "If you turn to your first handout you will see a poem. Mary would you please read it."

I followed along as Mary read, "Whispers in the Street" aloud.

They say they know what's best for me,
As we gather one and all.
They understand what's right and wrong for me,
Summer, winter, spring and fall.
They understand my every purpose,
They're caring and so sweet,
Life's evolving as predicted by
Those whispers in the street.

Those whispers, although silent
Shout a language all their own,
Passing from one another
Hearsay, which has been sown,
Changing lives which are so fragile,
Reaping harvests still unknown.

But why should I persist and listen,
To experts self-proclaimed?
Who know and predict the future,
As if it were prearranged.
But who gives these whispers their substance,
Determines their valid state?
It's a code, which has not been written
Yet determines people's fate.

Whispers which breed a generation,
Sending it on its way,
Whispers which create a dogma, but
Have nothing valid to say.
Yes, we've created an entire nation
Of citizens so discreet,
While marching to the beating drum
Of whispers in the street.

Whispers shouting boldly,
Demanding to be heard!
Giving substance to all rumors
Including those unheard,
Whispers, which control behavior
Of lives as yet unfurled.

Can anyone stand up and resist
Those whispers in the street?
Do you possess the strength and courage
To stand on your own two feet?
Do you dare to change and be different and
Oppose pretenders of the beat?
And rid this place of vicious lies,
Those whispers in the street?

My analytical mind began to look past the words to seek a deeper meaning of this poem. Since we're discussing consciousness it, obviously, must refer to it in some meaningful way.

"I think, therefore I am," Malachi interrupted, "five simple words that have had a monumental impact on the evolvement of the human condition. What makes this simple reasoning false, however, is the word 'I'. We have just discussed how we evolved from a Universal Consciousness out of a Universal Oneness. Universal implies all there is and it could, therefore, never include 'I' which describes a separate condition of self, a state of separation. This poem is all about ego! It's the ego, which guides us through our daily lives attempting to make a living and being successful. It's the ego that sews the seeds of separation blinding us to who we really are in the process."

Consciousness, I reasoned, is a gift of God. It is the thing, which began it all. Once God, the Universal Whole, became aware of Himself, He became conscious of Himself. Consciousness is awareness, awareness of self, and awareness of things around you, understanding of self, and understanding of things around you. Without consciousness there can be no thought. Without thought there can be no creation. Without creation there can be nothing, spiritual or material. Could the "big bang" then not be this cataclysmic explosion physicists presume created the universe, but rather the moment God became fully aware of Himself? Was this the moment the Universal Oneness became the Universal Consciousness?

I began to delve deeper into this concept looking for some kind of connection to help support my supposition. But does it really matter? More importantly, I believe, is the understanding that God's consciousness resides everywhere; it is omnipresent. Whether it began with the big bang or not is immaterial, the good news is we, and everything we see, are an expression having its origin in God's consciousness, thereby connecting us directly to the Universal Whole or the Universal Consciousness. For me, this was certainly a major breakthrough and I couldn't wait to pass my ideas by Malachi. Realizing the point when God became aware of Himself is not critical but, being He is aware of Himself now and we, through our awareness, are expressions of this Divine Being, opens a plethora of possibilities and opportunities. However you slice it, it seems we are one with God!

Yet consciousness cannot be so simply defined as an awareness having a direct and easy accessibility to the Universal Mind. Comparing our material existence to the world of spirit is like night and day. Our consciousness is dominated by the ego, an expression of self, deeming itself disconnected from everything else. There is no direct link from our individualized perception directly to God, certainly not for the non--enlightened like myself. Connecting to God, I reasoned, requires we connect to our inner self, the Biblical "mustard seed" of spiritual connection we have with the Universal Consciousness. Once we tap into its space we open up our inborn spiritual connection with the Kingdom of God.

Taking this realization a step further, God is Oneness with understanding and purpose. Without consciousness, understanding and purpose cannot exist. For who or what can understand and have purpose if it cannot realize it exists? Consciousness is a realization and understanding that "I am!" The "I am" is where consciousness began. Yet this "I am" is not singular in scope, instead encompassing all things as One Universal Whole. Was my reasoning correct? I raised my hand waiting to be recognized to speak.

"Yes Hans," Malachi asked.

"I have a theory and I'm wondering if it might have relevance?"

"Go ahead, Hans, let's hear it."

"OK, here it goes," as I began searching for words. It seemed like I was rambling at first as thoughts formed more quickly in my head than my ability to put them into words. Malachi interrupted a few times for clarification but, for the most part, he listened quietly resolved to let me ramble through my suppositions. After I finished there was long pause before he replied. I could see his furrowed brow while stroking his beard. My tale was either hogwash or it just might have some substance.

Finally the silence broke, "There's a lot there."

"I know."

"Consciousness is not an easy topic to define other than we all have it. Whether God became conscious at some point or always had self-awareness is, I don't think, important. The fact is He has it."

"Understand."

"The Indian mystic, Sadhguru, defines consciousness as a separate dimension unto itself, encompassing the entire universe. We are only instruments capable of accessing this consciousness and how deeply we're able to access it determines our material experience." He paused momentarily to see our reactions and continued, "What I really feel is important here is you touched on the subject of creation. Creation is, as you surmise, unavoidable. Whether knowingly or unknowingly, we all create at every moment of our lives. Creation is change. Evolution is change. Evolution is the creation of change."

"So I got that part right?"

Sounding encouraging, the old man continued, "You have a lot right. It must have taken you some time to come up with all of this?"

"It did," I replied.

"However, I think creation is the important thing. Consciousness does you no good if you don't use it to create; and a higher level of consciousness allows you to determine what you create."

"OK, I'm listening."

"It's a cause and effect thing," he continued "consciousness is the cause while creation is the effect. Or put another way, thought precedes the action."

"I see."

"Once consciousness was born," he began, "everything became possible. Creation became possible and once creation began it could not be stopped. Is evolution not the continuous process of creation? Is evolution therefore, not the trial and error method of improving, improving the self and improving one's surroundings? Improving knowingly with a specific purpose or mindfulness? These improvements are seen through change; change in species, change in environments, change in technology, change in understanding, change in science and so on. Change is inevitable because no two moments are alike. They may be similar, but never alike. With change comes evolution, whether progressing or regressing. But it always comes; it cannot be stopped, world without end. Therefore, creation, the inevitable byproduct of consciousness, becomes the bigger issue, and how we adapt to this constant change becomes the foremost question.

Creation can be either involuntary, such as through the forces of nature, or intended, such as the development of great cities. But creation is much more intimate. We have the ability to create because we are expressions of the Great Creator himself; we have the ability to "move mountains" through our inherent connection to the Universal Consciousness. All we need to do is understand the process and make it work for us. Failure to understand or ignore the process can be disastrous in our lives. Whether knowingly or not, we continuously create because our thoughts are at the root of the creative process."

"So if I wanted a million dollars all I have to do is think about it?" Paul interrupted.

"Basically," Malachi replied, "but it's not quite that simple. It takes passion and knowing to make things truly happen for you. Wishing and hoping will rarely do the trick. Also, you won't find a bag of cash on your front door either. The million dollars you desire will show up as an opportunity of some type needing to be recognized and taken hold of.

"In *The Evolution Angel*, Todd Michael identifies four steps in the process of mastering money:

"First, you want to embrace money with good, loving thoughts. Understand the money coming your way has been touched by the lives of many people. Respect money and honor it for what it is, a means for self and community improvement. It is not to be flaunted or used as a status symbol.

"Next, visualize an abundant supply of money coming your way and using it for the greater good. Hoarding money will disconnect the spiritual flow and defeat the purpose of the greater good.

"Third, express deep gratitude for everything you have received. Be a symbol for goodness with what you have received. With great monetary wealth comes a great responsibility to contribute to the greater common good.

"Finally, be a steward of goodness by watching the distribution of your wealth. Pay your debts and provide opportunities for those who need assistance. Give, give and give again. By recycling your acquired wealth, more will be attracted to you."

Moving on from money, Malachi continued to explain everything begins with consciousness, the awareness of self and everything around us. In the initial state of the "I Am" God became aware of himself. With an awareness of himself naturally came the recognition of his surroundings. For you cannot be aware of self without being knowledgeable of the environment around you. And this is where it all began, the big bang, the physical realm, the spiritual realm and all the other realms we are not aware of and do not understand.

Once consciousness surfaced every thing changed. The proverbial snowball turned into an avalanche. This avalanche is continuing to progress today. It will never stop. Consciousness will not allow it. For if creation stopped, consciousness would cease and, eventually, so would every physical and spiritual being because the infinite would then become finite.

But what preceded consciousness, or did it always exist? I felt myself going further down the proverbial rabbit hole knowing I would ultimately reach a place where there were no answers, at least ones I would understand. It was Joanne who broke the silence and pulled me back to my present reality, "But what about love? Isn't God loving and kind?"

"Yes," Malachi began, "within consciousness is love. Love is God. Love is everything. Love expresses itself through consciousness. Therefore, all things have their beginning with love. All things are begotten with purposeful Love. Love is at the center of all things. Love is the driving force that moves forward, which continues to express itself with perfection.

"To put it altogether, God is the Oneness from which all things emanate. God is the Oneness, the whole from which everything originates. Consciousness is God being aware of Himself. Consciousness is God's expression of love. Consciousness is the guiding force behind all creation, whether it is the Universal Oneness of God or whether it is the person working feverishly in the fields. Everything is driven by consciousness. For consciousness is not only a self-awareness, but also the awareness of one's surroundings. And with this awareness comes understanding, an understanding of why things are so. Consciousness is the 'I Am.' Consciousness is the force behind creation. Consciousness exists in every atom and every galaxy. For every thing is driven by God.

Everything is part of the omnipresence of God. God exists everywhere and so does his consciousness."

Malachi apologized for his apparent rambling but made sure to emphasize the creative process requires passion and a knowing things will come to pass. Creation begins with our thoughts; like seeds, those thoughts are brought to germination by our passion, the water of the creative process, and culminate in opportunities presenting themselves. It takes effort to create what you desire; it's not always an easy path. Creation begins with a thought, an idea, this idea is fed with a passion to succeed and a determination to bring it to fruition and finally it is created by doing, doing what is necessary to bring the idea to fruition.

The old man continued with a Biblical quote from Mark 11:22-24, "Have faith in God. For assuredly, I say to you, whoever says to this mountain, 'Be removed and be cast into the sea,' and does not doubt in his heart, but believes that those things he says will be done, he will have whatever he says. Therefore I say to you, whatever things you ask when you pray, believe that you receive them, and you will have them.'"

Looking around the classroom I could see five students hanging on every word Malachi spoke. I could imagine their thoughts racing at breakneck speeds threatening to explode in overdrive. It would, to be sure, take some time to assimilate all the things discussed today. If this was the first class, what would the last one be like? There were, I was sure, more enlightening lectures ahead that would, hopefully, culminate in defining who we really are.

It seemed like the class just started when Malachi concluded the day's lesson with an instruction to become more aware of our daily thoughts. "Thoughts have meaning and, more importantly, thoughts have creative power. Think wisely!"

I picked up my notes, still staring at nothing in particular, as my mind's engine roared along an unending expressway of thoughts. It was the first time I could remember thinking about what I was thinking. I barely heard Malachi's "Good bye" as I entered the hallway and headed to my car.

Chapter - 6

All Things God

"Abide in me, and I in you. As the branch cannot bear fruit
by itself, unless it abides in the vine, neither can you, unless you
abide in me. I am the vine; you are the branches. Whoever
abides in me and I in him, he it is that bears much fruit,
for apart from me you can do nothing."

(John 15:4-5)

Synchronicity is something I first read about in the *Celestine Prophesy* and if I'm not careful it will pass me by unnoticed. Karen and Tom contracted me almost a year ago to photograph their wedding at the Evergreen Lake House. I usually meet with my clients at the venue a week or two before the event to discuss specific details and to identify intimate photography locations. There was no way, however, I could have known about Malachi's shop being less than a mile away at the time the appointment was made and this time the synchronicity did not escape me.

As fall is always a picturesque time for weddings, I took this opportunity to photograph the lake's surrounding beauty. Nature's colors always add a bit of majesty to any landscape, especially when water reflections are involved. Lake Evergreen's calm waters, surrounded by junipers and spruce, were accentuated by yellow, white and purple wild flowers growing intermittently amongst their giant neighbors. Elk sauntered around the adjoining golf course separating the splendor of nature from the manmade beauty of sport, two different worlds merging into one scene of natural perfection.

Leaning on the rails of a bridge crossing a small creek I could see lovers gliding on the lake in their intimate paddleboats while others just laid out a blanket to read or to soak up the rays of an ever-present sun. Photographing places such as this was always a joy and invariably left me in a state of spiritual joyfulness, satisfying me for days.

Nestled just northeast of the intersection of Highway 73 and Colorado 74 lay the downtown area of Evergreen where I finished this photo tour by walking along its wooden sidewalks looking into one store window after another, occasionally entering to browse or to purchase a mouth-watering cone of chocolate ice cream while looking for Malachi's store. This time I decided to abandon the "Boardwalk" and turned left on Douglas Park Road, where I noticed a few more shops before spotting the small, corner store I was seeking. Inscribed on its window in circular fashion was "All Things God." He never gave us a definitive address that first day in class, but I was certainly glad to have found it. Just below the store's name was a symbol consisting of a red heart with its tip merging with the center of a purple infinity sign. I interpreted the sign to symbolize an eternal, loving God who was central to many of the world's religions. This God symbol was encircled by people holding hands in a universal representation of brotherhood. With my curiosity in overdrive, I headed for the front door with great anticipation. A bell, singing like wind chimes blowing in the breeze, announced my presence.

"Hello," I called out as I entered, "is anyone home?"

Startled, Malachi looked up from his book, obviously surprised to see me in spite of the bell announcing my presence, "Yes, yes, welcome. Please come in. Hans, if I remember correctly? What brings you to this part of town?"

"I just had a meeting with a couple whose wedding I'll be photographing at the Lake House in a couple of weeks. And you mentioned in class that you had a store in Evergreen so I figured I'd check it out."

"Well, I'm glad you did. This store is all about God. Everything you will find here has a spiritual message taking you one step closer to realizing who you really are. It's a message frightening to some people but, I assure you, there is nothing to fear and there's something here for everyone. Let me assure you, your visit here is no accident. You're here for a reason and that reason will find you."

Hesitating while digesting his remarks, I began looking around the room and saw three aisles before me with shelves overflowing with books, souvenir type trinkets, crystals and even some clothes, most lying in an unruly and random fashion without any noticeable organization. "Where do I start?"

"Anywhere you like, whatever you were meant to find will find you."

Continuing to be puzzled by his remarks, I walked forward with no particular target in mind. Of the three aisles before me, I opted to go down the center one for no specific reason other than it seemed to be a good place to start. Malachi was not as talkative as he was in class and it seemed he was more inclined to let me search for whatever attracted me. "If you have any questions about anything, just ask."

"Thanks, will do."

The items on the shelves weren't overly impressive, most resembled a variety of souvenirs I had seen in most of the stores along the "Boardwalk." Trinkets, personifying the town of Evergreen and the state of Colorado, dominated the inventory and appeared out of place in a shop professing to be all about God. How they could characterize a spiritual message seemed a bit far-fetched. I was expecting something more profound and personal. "Do you have anything of a more spiritual nature, something different?"

"Just keep going down the aisle, those souvenirs help pay the monthly rent. Close your eyes and tap into your inner self. What you seek will find you."

Stopping momentarily I closed my eyes and took a deep breath. It didn't take long before I was subliminally directed to the middle of the first aisle. Retracing my steps, I walked down the aisle stopping near the middle where I saw a series of items calling out to me. I caught a glimpse of a globe, more like a hologram, of what looked like the universe with a hammer looking like it belonged to Thor lying next to it.

"What exactly are you looking for?" the old man, having somehow quietly approached behind me, asked.

"I'm not really sure, " I replied, "possibly something to help me understand what God is all about."

"That's a tall order! Not that God is difficult to understand, but, all too often, our egos get in the way and cloud the God waters. How do you view Him?"

I could feel my cheeks turn a crimson color as I searched for a satisfactory answer, "I've always viewed Him as out there, somewhere, looking over us in a protective way." I wondered where this might go and, like in class, Malachi did not disappoint.

"The good thing," Malachi began, "is that all roads lead to God. There is no right or wrong way. Whatever road we travel, whatever belief system we embrace and whatever, if any, God we proclaim, eventually we'll all arrive at the same place."

"What about heaven and hell?" I asked.

"Most people believe they are physical places where souls of the dearly departed go to spend eternity based on their deeds in this material world. I, for one, believe they are states of consciousness, created by us and ingrained into our psyche by doctrines and dogmas over the course of hundreds of years. I will leave you be for now, just remember what was meant for you will call out to you."

Both the global hologram, which seemed to project the attribute of omnipresence, and the hammer which reminded me of Thor, the Norse God of thunder and lightning and Marvel Studio's protector of mankind, certainly called out to me. To me, the hammer signified God's attribute of being all-powerful and His ability to do whatever he wants! No place was this more evident than in the story of creation; on day one He created light; on day two He created the firmament; on day three He created the earth, sea and vegetation; on day four

He created the sun, moon and stars; on day five He created the birds and sea animals; on day six He created the land animals and humans. "God," *The Urantia Book* states, "is unlimited in power, divine in nature, final in will, infinite in attributes, eternal in wisdom, and absolute in reality."

When I picked up the hammer it felt light, like a feather, almost having no weight at all. Inscribed on one side was the word "Omnipotence," and on the other side was a spiritual passage from the book of Isaiah:

> I make known the end from the beginning,
> From ancient times, what is still to come.
> I say, "My purpose will stand,
> And I will do as I please.
> From the east I summon a bird of prey,
> From a far-off land, a man to fulfill my purpose.
> What I have said, that I will bring about;
> What I have planned, that I will do.
>
> (Isaiah 46:10-11)

It was then I realized omnipotence is not about physical strength at all, but strength of character and values. Personal resolve and determination are the catalysts behind success or failure. As Jesus said, "With man this is impossible, but with God all things are possible." (Mat 19:26) It was then I realized the real power behind omnipotence is creation.

Placing the hologram and hammer in my basket, I turned around to find a representation of omniscience. The old man came up behind me, smiling while handing me a book. "Here, if you're going to take the items of omnipresence and omnipotence, you will surely want a book about omniscience, it's called *Knowing All Things*. I was reading it when you entered the store." Taking it from him I was struck by the Leonardo da Vinci quote on the front cover, "The knowledge of all things is possible."

It was certainly a book worthy of those found by Harry Potter in the stores along Diagon Alley. On the first page was a quote from Socrates, "I cannot teach anybody anything. I can only make them think." It was followed by Psalm 139:1-4:

> You have searched me, Lord,
> And you know me.
> You know when I sit and when I rise;
> You perceive my thoughts from afar.
> You discern my going out and my lying down;
> You are familiar with all my ways.
> Before a word is on my tongue
> You, Lord, know it completely.

As I sifted through the pages, I began to realize the book appeared to have no ending. Try as I might, I could never get to the last page. "Why is there no end to this book?"

"Ah," came the reply, "If you've heard of Wilford Woodruff, former president of The Church of Jesus Christ of Latter-day-Saints, then you must realize that 'God Himself is increasing and progressing in knowledge, power, and dominion, and will do so, worlds without end.' Just as we continue to learn, God continues to grow."

"But I thought that God already knows everything, past, present and future?" "Yes, but God only lives in the now, there is no past or future with God. The question then becomes as we learn and grow does God grow as well, or is our learning just a process of us awakening to what He knows? But, learning is not only understanding what is written in books, it also involves tangible and intangible things such as emotions. The fact the book has no ending should answer your question. However you want to look at it, God knows everything there is to know, NOW!"

Stunned, I quickly replied, "But if the book is continuing to grow, how come it's not getting any heavier?"

"Knowledge is mental and acquiring knowledge is a cerebral endeavor. There is never any weight associated with the processes of knowing and comprehension. The weight of knowledge is in one's ability to understand and apply what one has learned to everyday life. It is both a mental and emotional activity, never a physical undertaking. What you feel is the binding of the book, the wisdom contained therein is weightless and timeless." Shaking my head and smiling back at the old man, I placed the book in my basket. He patted my shoulder and walked back to his desk by the front door.

As I left the shop I could see Malachi smile and wave at me through the window. He had a knowing look on this face, knowing I would be back. I waved back and quickly walked to my car, as I didn't want to traverse Denver's highway system during rush hour. It wasn't until I reached the entrance ramp of Interstate 70, after turning off the radio, that I began to mentally relive my visit to Evergreen. The photo shoot was calming and creative with a variety of shots attempting to capture peace, tranquility and, as best as I could, spirituality; but surely my trip's highlight was visiting Malachi's shop.

God's attributes had been taught to me while I was attending confirmation classes at Bethany Lutheran Church during my junior high school years in Queens, New York. It was Pastor Bischoff who attempted to explain God's omnipresence, omnipotence and omniscience, but it never really resonated with me. It was difficult enough to imagine an all-powerful Deity, but to include attributes of being all knowing and all-present was beyond my ability to perceive how such abilities could apply to this every day world. My teenage mind was not ready for such deep reasoning and so I simply accepted these facts from ministers who certainly knew more and were better educated than I was. These beliefs remained with me, unshaken, for the better part of my life. However, my visit with the old man made me think and question my impatient approval of concepts I didn't quite comprehend.

What exactly is meant by the omnipresence of God is the question I first formulated in my mind. If omnipresence, quite simply, means he's everywhere, then there cannot be a place where He is not. But my understanding throughout the years has been that God is next to me, or looking at me from above, albeit invisible. But if He were everywhere, then He would have to be in every molecule that exists, and not just every molecule, but every atom or even quark.

These things I could accept, despite the many questions they raised. But if He is everywhere, in every existing molecule, doesn't it mean he is in every cell of my body? And if it is so, doesn't it mean I am an extension of God, I am a part of God and He is a part of me? This simple deductive reasoning seemed much too easy for such a deep perception. Is this what people meant by proclaiming to be an extension of God? And as this extension, do I also have all the qualities of God? Am I also a great creator? Am I also a spiritual being of love? What am I? Who am I?

Putting these questions aside, I returned to concepts easier to understand. It appeared to me the real difference between God and myself is simple; He is everywhere in Spirit, whereas I am here in body. As Spirit He is not relegated to one place and can be everywhere at once. But what is Spirit? Is Spirit not individualized as well? Haven't people with near death experiences met up with their deceased loved ones in the spiritual world? Is that not individualized spirit? So where does the omnipresence come in?

Passing the Floyd Hill exit, I failed to see the sign alerting drivers of the six percent downhill grade for the next six miles, forcing me to step on my brake as the speedometer began to pass eighty just as my car sped by the runaway truck ramp. It wasn't until I reached Morrison, another delightful town in the foothills of the Rockies, where the highway began to level out and my exit drew near. Merging onto E-470 I resumed exploring thoughts that lingered for the last few miles.

Continuing my struggle with omnipresence, I returned to the idea we are individualized expressions of God. I came to terms that God is everywhere on the conscious level and His awareness is not only everywhere but within us as well. Just as we humans are the materialized expressions of spirit, we are also the conscious expression of God.

Consciousness is everywhere; it has to be if God is truly omnipresent. God is conscious of his awareness, just as we are conscious of our own awareness. We are conscious of all things going on around us, just as God is conscious of all existing around him. The difference is of scale; God is universal while we are limited to our environment. We are incapable of understanding the vastness of our world, much rather the vastness of the universe and understanding the realm of spirit.

Suddenly feeling philosophical, I reasoned it is our limited knowledge of consciousness that inhibits all we are all capable of. We are locked in a daily struggle of survival and relationships in whatever we do. This struggle inhibits our ability to see beyond our needs; it inhibits our ability to see beyond our physical world. For how can we expect to understand the nonphysical when we don't fully understand our own existence and purpose?

Man's perception of reality is limited in this physical realm. He, because of his needs, is unwilling to open himself up freely to God. Since God is present in every microscopic cell in the universe, man only needs to open himself up to God and he will not be in need. Jesus is the one person who walked the earth who was able to do this. He was the great example. So why is it so difficult for us?

We, in a sense, are our own worst enemies. We are taught and have been influenced since childhood about how and in what direction our lives should go. We are influenced in the ways of societal expectancies. We are taught we must fend for ourselves if we are to persevere. To persevere, we must establish ourselves in this material world and look for material things to make our lives bearable and successful.

We lose our spiritual consciousness with which we enter the world. But it is not lost, it can be found deep within us. It is there for us to access whenever we want. It is there where the consciousness of God resides within us. It is there where we need to look to grow our lives beyond the restrictive physical realm.

God is with everyone and everything in consciousness. Every atom that exists is an expression of God's consciousness. Every life, every thought, every action is an expression of God. He knows it, unfortunately we don't.

God was beginning to make sense. Once I began to better understand the concept of omnipresence, the attributes of omnipotence and omniscience became easier to understand; God is everywhere, so it stands to reason He would be all powerful and all knowing. Thor's hammer was, for me, the physical symbol of God's strength and power as it had been presented in many Biblical stories. Just then a vision of Malachi appeared in my subconscious reminding me that, "In the beginning God created the heavens and earth." Thinking about his intrusion for a few seconds, I came to the realization, in spite of the numerous Biblical wars and battles, God's power lies in His ability to create, not destroy. Creation is the real power and its power is not solely limited to God; we, by our very nature as expressions of the Almighty, are creative beings as well.

Realizing there was probably more to God's "Omni" attributes than I could fathom at this time, I, nevertheless, felt satisfied I had come to a determination which not only made sense but was developed through my own limiting filters this life furnished me. Amazingly, I was coming up on the I-25 interchange amid decreased mental jousting, not fully realizing how I had reached this point so quickly. Navigating the last ten to fifteen miles seemed like the car had been put on autopilot; I couldn't remember passing the Chatfield Reservoir or the construction beginning near the Santa Fe Drive exit. Yet I could recall my internal discussion without hesitation. Grasping I may not have been fully in control of my vehicle for the last few miles, I quickly disbanded my cerebral activity and continued home, uninterrupted, anxious to see what my new souvenirs were all about.

Parking the car, I rushed into the house. I called out to Jannette but received no reply and, making myself comfortable on the sofa, proceeded to examine my new items. I pulled out the global hologram labeled "The Sphere of All There Is." Holding it in my hand I turned it around and around until it became warmer to the touch. Closing my eyes, I focused all my energy on the hologram and slowly a vision formed in my mind.

Opening before me was a sea of stars and galaxies rotating and moving in all different directions. I could tell that the red shifting ones were moving further away while the blue shifting ones were coming closer. A vision of Psalm 139:7-10 appeared out of nowhere:

Where can I go from Your Spirit?
Or where can I flee from Your presence?
If I ascend to heaven, You are there;
If I make my bed in Sheol, behold, You are there.
If I take the wings of the dawn,
If I dwell in the remotest part of the sea,
Even there Your hand will lead me,
And Your right hand will lay hold of me.

A message from Malachi then entered my subconscious mind, "This hologram represents God's omnipresence. If you slide the arrow on the left you will see a greater sample and meaning of His all-beingness."

"Thanks," I replied to an empty room, wondering how he knew what I was looking at, as I quickly located the arrow swiping it to the left. This was not a simple hologram, but a digital holographic representation of several images. The next visual seemed like an infinite number of trees and flowers stretching into all directions. The flowers were so colorful and vivid, I could feel the urge to reach out and touch them. The screen could be rotated easily with my finger to bring different landscapes into focus, almost like a 360-degree panorama. It was not only a three-dimensional picture but it also heightened my sense of smell and touch.

There was another arrow and I swiped it to the left, revealing a group of animals and birds grazing peacefully on a wide, endless savanna. There were zebras and wildebeests with small birds on their backs picking annoying ticks from their host's dusty hides. Suddenly their heads perked up as carnivores approached from a distance. This was no longer a simple hologram but a 3-D video of life on the African plains. I rotated the screen and the scene changed to an underwater ballet of hundreds of fish swimming in and around a vast structure of coral. The colorful fish stayed near their protective barriers as predators were lurking in the open waters. While life appeared to be peacefully idyllic, danger, it seemed, was never far away.

I flicked another arrow to the left and a panorama of a major city appeared with people and traffic moving all around. This environment was more stressful than the previous ones and displayed some of the stressors people place upon themselves. Having spent more than twenty years working in the bowels of Manhattan, it was a lifestyle I could relate to. Commuting, traffic-jams, deadlines and expectations were only a few of the strains society placed on its members. Being in a peaceful mindset, I flicked the next arrow to the left.

What appeared was a mirror; I was looking at a reflection of myself. When I attempted to rotate the screen the image became less visible until it disappeared entirely. Further swiping of the screen brought my reflection back. This was the last layer of the hologram as the next swipe brought me back to the star and galaxy visual. Before I could shut if off, a short poem appeared on the screen:

> When I look in the mirror, what do I see?
> A reflection of Spirit looking back at me.
> It cannot touch, it cannot feel,
> But its Truth and Love are eternally real.
> Awaken now and reach for your star,
> Embrace the one who you really are.

And in my mind I could hear Malachi shouting with glee, "God is here. He is always here. He is never there!" And he continued with a Paul Ferrini quote, " God is beyond these limits, for He is without form. Being formless, He abides in all things. There is no place where His presence cannot be found...As a non-limited presence, His Spirit moves through our minds and our experience. We draw our very

Essence from this presence...Bodies seem to make you separate from one another, but Divine Essence unites you."

I instantly found myself in touch with my inner self, realizing I held within my hand all there is, an assortment of stars and dust and planets; a combination of all things animate and inanimate; a globe of eternal proportions, of unmatched beauty and unimaginable wealth; an orb filled with infinite wisdom and unbridled love. It is God.

Within this globe, I exist. Within this globe my brother and sister exist. Within this globe all the entities of the heavens and all the beasts of the earth exist. Here exist the plains and the mountains and the waters of our mother earth. Here, we the people exist in a Oneness called God.

Here God has provided all there is to want, all there is to need, all that exists within this great Oneness. The Almighty has given us freedom of choice; regardless of our individualized choices we'll never sever the ties binding us to the Love permeating our physical bodies and environment. The Almighty knows our spiritual bonds can never be broken. Spiritual chains of love, not the physical chains of burden, bind us; we are bound by the spiritual bonds of goodness, not by the physical bonds of desire; we are bound by spiritual freedom not physical oppression. Instantly, my internal instincts swelled to the point of bursting as I reached heavenward in prayer:

Awaken us, O Lord, not as individuals in need, but as a conglomerate of universal brotherhood, sharing and lifting one another to unimaginable success possible only through togetherness. Awaken us to the unlimited possibilities awaiting us at your table where every being is welcomed to feast in your goodness, in your joy and in your love. Awaken us to the universal peace existing within all of us. Awaken us to the realization that Love does not need, Love does not desire, Love is and always will be.

In closing I recognize your love is what binds us together in one big melting pot of black and white, of yellow and red, of brown and gray, of rich and poor, of Christian and Hebrew and Muslim and Hindu. Combine this pot of all separate classes we have created, stir this pot with your Godly love and extract a mankind of eternal brotherhood where everyone is equal, where no one is cast into the shadows and no one is more important than another. Replace our blinders of race and religion with the sunshine of love and goodness.

Thank you! Thank you! Thank you!

Your love and wisdom usurps all and will forever cast away the robe of indignities, which covers this planet. Thank you for lifting the veil of darkness, as we are reborn in the basking sunshine of togetherness. Join us in a Godly embrace of the I Am.

It is with Knowing I release this prayer, it is with Knowing I open my heart to the realization, "For nothing is impossible with God." Let the winds of change declare a new, eternal mantra of forgiveness and love to the four corners of the universe. I release this message of good news with a declaration, shouting at the top of my lungs, "I Am, I Am, I Am!"
And so it is. Amen.

Chapter - 7

Tick, Tock

"Yours is a temporary existence, your reality is everlasting Spirit."
—Spirit

"Today we will talk about time. What does that have to do with God, one might ask? Well, time is the great divider between our physical world and the spiritual world of God." Malachi looked around the room for a moment before continuing, "What is your concept of time, Paul?"

"Well, time is the sequencing of events that happen in our daily lives."

"OK, how about you, Mary. What is time to you?"

"It's a means of organizing and planning our lives, by putting things in order. I guess it's pretty much what Paul just said."

"Good, and you, Joanne?"

"I see it as a concept of change having its own measurement such as days, hours and seconds."

"So how do you measure the Now? Does the Now have a component of time?"

"Yes, but when you really get down to it, it's very miniscule."

"OK, Sarah, what do you think?"

"According to A Course In Miracles, time is an illusion. It exists only in our perceived material world."

"So, we are the creators of time?"

"Yes."

"Hans, what do you think?"

"Time is an objective concept that doesn't exist in the spiritual world."

"Very good. None of you are entirely wrong. But does it really matter? Our bodies age regardless of what we do, in fact everything around us ages as well. It seems our physical world is encumbered by time while our consciousness has the freedom to escape the structure of time. Yes, time, as we know it, has structure. There are hours and days and years, all of which are measured very precisely. Yet, our consciousness has no boundaries of time, as we are free to think whatever we want without any restrictions whatsoever, including time.

"In *Love Without Conditions*, Paul Ferrini states, 'Let go of the past, and you will have no grievances...Time makes the wound seem real. Time makes life seem real. It makes death seem real. It makes all the changes that happen in your life seem real. Yet none of these are real...If you could be without time for a single instant...you would understand your salvation. In that timeless moment...there is just the moment of pure being, of non-separateness, of non-judgment.' It seems to me that time is an albatross around our necks dragging us further into the world of separation."

"But without time the world would be chaotic. There would be no semblance of order or cohesion between people and nations," Paul interrupted.

"That may be true here in our physical world where judgments, laws and dogmas separate rather than unite. But is that our true reality? Or are we spiritual beings guided by Love?"

"Love overcomes everything, including time," Sarah blurted out, stopping Malachi short.

"Expand on that, won't you Sarah?"

"True Love, not the love we experience here, overcomes everything, judgment, hatred and sin in general. When we're in a state of Love we are in a state of Oneness with God. Here there is no concept of time because time is a form of separation and Love casts us in the everlasting moment of Now."

"Excellent, Sarah, I couldn't have said it better myself. It all comes down to who you think you really are! Therein lies your dichotomy! Are you mortal man or immortal Spirit?"

Again, Malachi's eyes went skyward as if he were reading messages on the ceiling; all eyes followed his attempting to see what was going on. "Excuse me," he interrupted as all eyes left an empty ceiling and re-focused on the man at the front of the room, "I was just thinking how God is perceived. Does He have a presence in the past or future, or is He constantly in the present, the Now? The Bible states, 'In the time of my favor I heard you, and in the day of salvation I helped you. I tell you now is the time of God's favor, now is the day of salvation.' That's from 2 Corinthians 6:2. In *Living as God*, Stewart states, 'The now does not move. Linear time is illusory. In this context, time is best understood as being vertical, not horizontal, holding every potential simultaneous in the now, awaiting our decision as to what we want to experience. Any belief that we cannot experience something is the mind's limitation, not of the One Self. And we can choose to experience the same thing as many times as we wish.' As you can hopefully see, time is a great separator. It removes us from the only place where we can truly know God, which is the Now."

Our mind is a chatterbox I thought, unable to fully concentrate on anything for over a few hours. It is constantly in a state of turmoil reliving moments of the past and planning for hopeful new adventures. Most often we fail to realize the most important moment is now, the moment when everything happens.

We look forward with hope to rekindle those past moments filled with excitement and adventure. Sure, our memories can reincarnate a small sample of emotional splendor of times past, but those moments do not last long and are gone in a few instants to, hopefully, be relived again at some future time. However, memories are truly fleeting and rarely reincarnate.

Likewise, we cannot speed future plans into our present. Carefully intended plans, hinging on some likely events or happenings, which have not yet come to fruition, often cause our minds to drift out of the present. This creates a sense of hope, a condition that will never exist in the realm of Spirit.

One of our greatest mistakes comes when we continue to wander between states of what happened and what will be without stopping in the place of what is. The present is not a fleeting moment disappearing in the past, but rather, it is a state of being. The present, despite the fact we continually attempt to diminish its importance, is everlasting.

The past no longer matters, the future will always be a moment away, but the present is always here. Interestingly enough, our physical body is glued to the present moment for it can never travel forward or backwards through time. It is the mind, driven by ego, which resurrects or imagines future events through psychological or emotional filters. Physically, however, we can never leave the moment of Now. Consciousness is, it never was or ever will be! It is only our ego, drifting out of the Now, which attempts to reincarnate a coveted past or create an aspiring opportunity. There is never any peace along the ego's path of hope and anticipation, only turmoil and confusion. Real inner peace can only be found in the moment of Now.

Everything happens in the present. Nothing ever happens in the future and the past can never be recaptured. Yet, as people with chatterbox minds, we tend to exert most of our mental energy in places having no meaning while ignoring the only thing that matters: the Now.

It was Mary's furrowed brow which gave away her internal struggle when she asked, "So how does one live in the Now without being caught up in a world of promises and regrets? How does one continue to focus on those people or things in our present condition without falling off a cliff into the pits of past and future?"

Malachi was quick to respond, "The Now is not just simply the present moment, but it is also the moment of the I Am. Now is the only moment that defines you! Now is never a moment of I was or I will be. I Am is not only the moment of Now, but it also defines who you are. I am God, or I am something else; worse yet is having absolutely no idea of what or who you are for it will ensure continued struggles with your present condition.

"As Paul Ferrini also writes, 'Authentic spirituality is not linear...If you could be without time for a single instant...you would understand your salvation.' There is only one moment and one understanding bringing joy and happiness to your present condition: I am God! Remember, God is! God never was and never will be. Being firmly entrenched in a place of love and peace and joy is all we could ever hope for. We continually encounter stresses and obstacles attempting to reach those very states of success. We search, never quite understanding what we're looking for or, worse yet, where to find it. Our busy minds, blinded by events around us and emotions within, keep us searching in a material world, which has no answers. It is a dichotomy most people never recognize or know exists. Who are you? Are your roots human flesh and blood, or are your roots spiritual?

"Our world does not exist out there somewhere; it exists within us. Our world has its roots in our spiritual soul connection to the Universal Divine, regardless of how hard we try to deny it. Therefore, the secret is not having to connect with God outside of us, the secret is to connect with our God center residing within us. Connecting to our inner self ensures our connection to God. In fact, this connection already exists; we only have to become aware of it. We are connected to God every single moment of every single day. Realizing this makes the past and future irrelevant; there can never be a better moment than Now."

Malachi reminded us the mind never stops, as one thought is replaced by another. So how does one overcome its constant interruptions and seemingly important directives? It starts with a breath! Taking a deep breath slows down the thoughts racing through your head. Then take another, and another. Breathing slows the metabolism and, in turn, slows the activity of our ever-present ego. Slow the mind and find your way. Only by calming the ego can we hope to venture into our internal God space and connect with an unparalleled state of being, a state of love missing in our material world. This is what connecting with one's inner self is all about. Connect with your very soul and nothing else matters. The past magically disappears and the future can never promise a better tomorrow. What's left is your present condition of bliss, the Now.

"Change your mind, change the world! You have entered the 'Twilight Zone' where time doesn't exist, or, at least, it doesn't matter. Your state of bliss is the only thing concerning you. So firmly will you be entrenched in this state of being, time will have no meaning. Time ceases to exist! All that matters is your present condition. You are in the presence of God! Better yet, you are God incarnate!

"Within you," Malachi continued, "are two opposing forces, one self-created, constantly pulling you in opposite directions. The self-created ego is the devil who blinds you with ideals based on competition, need and power. One's inner self, lying quietly dormant, sends intuitive messages, often ignored, to help guide you in the direction of building self-worth and connecting with your spiritual soul. Unfortunately, most of us listen to the one who screams the loudest. Those cries drown out the inner calls for peace and quiet. Screams offer short-term rewards and notoriety, but they do not last long and need to be replenished often. Those screams keep you searching for new and better things to fill your treasure chest of life accomplishments. Is it any wonder one is never satisfied? In the race between the tortoise and the hare, the ego is the proverbial rabbit.

"Take away the past and the future, Malachi continued, "and time no longer exists. It ceases to have meaning. Immersed in a constant state of Now erases the need to look back or the hope of a better tomorrow. Now is the only thing important and Now triumphs over time, in fact it erases the concept of time entirely. Why is this important? Because once we become truly immersed in the state of Now, then we can truly embrace the presence of God. God knows nothing of what was left behind or what is waiting for us, He does not care; He does not care about your failures or your dreams; He does not understand your need for remembrances or hopes; His everything is there in this precious moment. There is no need, there is no want, there is no regret; there is only unbridled love, joy and peace. Why would anyone want to venture from such an existence and embrace the uncertainty created by a moment of time? Throughout our lives we travel the maze of yesterday and tomorrow, searching for our final goal, the Now."

Malachi stopped momentarily to see if any questions were being pondered. Receiving only blank stares and silence, he continued, "To be quite honest, we can live nowhere else but in the Now, regardless how hard we try. In our humanity, however, mankind has devised an imaginative way of measuring progress by inventing a past and future. It is an ingenious way for the ego to maintain control of our actions. By remembering certain events or intending certain actions, our ego imprisons our mind by instilling hope or reawakening memories thus forcing our focus from the very place where creation occurs. The prison of the ego contains no walls nor are there any bars in its windows; it is firmly constructed within the confines of the mind through the manipulation of thought. But don't ever sell it short. Its ability to incarcerate is every bit as powerful as the highest walls of the land. Unlike the judicial system administering laws, sentences imposed by the ego are self-imposed and, quite often, more cruel and unjust than those societal laws invented in the first place. Separation is the greatest imposed sentence man has enforced upon himself!

"While legal incarceration is predicated on unwanted behavior and administered for a predetermined amount of time, the ego fills our thoughts with judgment, doubt and uncertainty leading us to question the very foundation of our being. There can be no greater proof of this than its concocted idea of separation. By creating the illusion of separation we are overmatched by the ego's continued attack on the very core of who we are. Unfortunately, this permanent prison sentence can only be remedied with our demise. While 'time heals all wounds,' it only does so when we come to the realization time is a fabrication and doesn't exist. There is only one existence: the Now! That existence only manifests itself in the I Am!"

It was a powerful ending to a powerful session, which at times seemed more like a sermon than a class. Regardless, Malachi had made his point: time is an enemy aiding and abetting our separation from God. The alarm clock signaling a new day is actually increasing our sense of separation.

After class I decided to look at Malachi's book of omniscience, *Knowing All Things*, to see whether it addressed the concept of time. Paging through the book, I arrived to page 345, a chapter called "Tick, Tock." It began, auspiciously enough with a poem:

> The comfort of darkness sustains the soul,
> For outside fears are unknown.
> Its slumbering journey will soon come to pass,
> When it will have to survive on its own.
>
> The wisdom of time will always be there
> Though it will waver more often than not.
> It must learn anew, it can't recollect
> As memories of past have long been forgot.
>
>
> Floating in air like the fish neath the sea,
> The soul's awakened with unbridled fright,
> No longer secure and surrounded by fuss
> And blinded by bright, vibrant light.
>
> How it got here the soul doesn't know,
> Nor recalls where it came from.
> From this moment on all things have been changed,
> Its journey through time has begun.

Tick, tock. Tick, tock.

According to the poem, it appears time is a component of the material world, beginning when we are born. I began to reminisce about my earlier days and how difficult it must have been to raise a child in the shadows of World War II.

My entry into the world of time had an inauspicious beginning. It was almost 75 years ago when I came to terms with that bright, vibrant light. The war had ended less than a year before and my parents' prayers of survival from bullets were replaced by ones for sustenance. Food was scarce enough without the rationing which made raising a baby much more difficult. Prayers were fortunately answered when my father landed a job at the American military base and occasionally brought home a slab of bacon, or bread or beef tied around his legs or waist so as not to get caught stealing. Tears shed for the safe return of family only a year earlier were replaced by tears of hope for food and survival.

> The year is 1946.
> Mothers have stopped crying,
> Nations have stopped mourning,
> A new generation is born.
> The year is 1946.
>
> A new human outlook is upon us.
> Political hatred has been overcome,
> At the cost of 45 million souls.
> The year is 1946.
>
> A worldwide rebuilding has begun,
> Churches and schools and homes,
> Road and bridges and lives,
> But most of all lives.
> The year is 1946.

A new awareness is born,
About individual rights
And national pride;
About equality and purpose,
About the emergence of the soul,
The year is 1946.

Tears have cleansed dirty faces.
Families have buried their lost.
Brick by brick cities have begun
To rebuild.
A new age is dawning.
The year is 1946.

I thought again how my parents didn't speak much about God, perhaps out of frustration or the long ago loss of hope. Along with the carnage of the war years, prayers were often discarded along the roadside, forgotten and abandoned by people lost in a world turned upside down. An all-powerful God, it seems, was ill equipped to deal with the hatred and prejudices created by those He created in His image. But the war was over and it was time to move on, it was time, as Morgan Freeman so poignantly stated in the Shawshank prison yard to "get busy living or get busy dying." The Byrds put into music this Biblical quote from Ecclesiates 3:1-8:

a time to be born and a time to die,
a time to plant and a time to uproot,
a time to kill and a time to heal...
a time to weep and a time to laugh,

Tick, tock. Tick, tock.

Regardless of my inauspicious beginning, here I was in 2020, approaching the closing stages of my life, still searching for an identity. My name, I understand, is Hans Benes, a person who has gone through life attempting to be the best person possible. Life has been like a rollercoaster, a series of ups and downs. Change, I have learned, is the only constant. With each tick of the clock, one fleeting moment is replaced by another as time, unabated, moves forever forward, unaffected and uncaring about what is happening in my life or, for that matter, in anyone else's. Like a big, well-oiled machine life's big jigsaw puzzle marches to completion. How often has it been when I've asked this train of life to stop and take a rest? How often have I asked for it to stop and let me take a do over for ill choices made out of haste or want? But like an exquisitely engineered Swiss clock, life moves ever forward.

There have been good times and times of struggle, there has been laughter and the shedding of tears, and there has been the joy of birth and the agony of death. Life has never been professed as easy, nor has it ever followed a straight and narrow path where events were easily addressed and solved. Life is tantamount to a roller coaster ride, whose ups and downs often help us grow in understanding, empathy and forgiveness. Time is the great teacher! It teaches us to fear, to love, to compete, to grow, to laugh, to cry and to forgive. Time teaches us to look back at lessons learned and to look forward to new journeys and new beginnings.

Tick, tock! Tick, tock!

Unfortunately, many of the lessons time lays before us go unfulfilled or, all too often, unrecognized. Throughout history, mankind has been besieged with wars, disease and famine; events, which could have been avoided through a bond of brotherhood, often lie broken and withered in the deep chasm of human dreams. Events, both natural and man-made, have often served to alienate the world populace instead of bringing them together; conflicts primarily serve to establish dominance and force compliance while famine and need often provide a roadmap for self-serving economic wealth and fiscal power. Lost are the lessons of equality, brotherhood and spiritual oneness. Time, the great teacher, is mostly misunderstood or underestimated by our acceptance of separation and need. Time, it seems, has created a lineage of people who are more inclined to march to individual ideals, thereby creating separate societies bonding through race, religion or politics; societies serving to exclude and judge based on their own prejudices.

Old sayings proclaim, "Time heals all wounds," and, "This too shall pass." These old proverbs identify change as the only constant. Change is inevitable as one moment is replaced by another; the body grows older by the minute, needs change by the season and wisdom changes over the course of years. In this temporal world we are gifted with being able to re-evaluate our past and plan our future, but we rarely stop to enjoy the present.

But now Spirit is asking me to let go, let go of all the baggage weighing me down and keeping me from my appointed goal, whatever it may be. Trust! This is indeed a difficult concept for a person who always seems to have visions of process and obstacles long before the journey begins. As a result, beginnings of new endeavors are scattered around the house waiting to be re-discovered. It is, quite literally, a task of picking up the pieces. How they all fit together is my current jigsaw puzzle wherein I may find the purpose I am looking for. I have the insight from my Spiritual Guide to just let go and that better days lie ahead. Let the journey begin.

Tick, tock. Tick, tock.

This book of omniscience appeared to be a means of self-introspection of my life and all the events influencing my current condition. It was almost like a Freudian trip into the past. A further discussion about the concepts of time was found on page 1946.

But what exactly is time? Is it just the natural progression from one event to another, thereby creating with it the past, present and future? Carlo Lovelli, in his principal work *The Order of Time*, gives us this insight, "And hence this is what time is: it is entirely in the present in our minds, as memory and as anticipation." Saint Augustine gave it a bit more clarity when he stated:

> "If future and past events exist, I want to know where they are. If I have not the strength to discover the answer, at least I know that wherever they are, they are not there as future or past, but as present. For if there also they are future, they will not yet be there. If there also they are past, they are no longer there. Therefore, wherever they are, whatever they are, they do not exist except in the present."

What is clear to me, is that time is something we created to map out a progression through this material plane; while we spend an inordinate amount of time remembering and planning, we can never forget it is only the present having an impact on us. While it makes some sense to me, Augustine, nevertheless, goes on to muddy the waters further when he stated:

> "If we can think of some bit of time which cannot be divided into even the smallest instantaneous moments, that alone is what we can call 'present.' And this time flies so quickly from future into past that it is an interval with no duration. If it has duration, it is divisible into past and future. But the present occupies no space."

In his brilliant work *The Power of Now: A Guide to Spiritual Enlightenment*, Eckhart Tolle states, "Time isn't precious at all, because it is an illusion. What you perceive as precious is not time but the one point that is out of time: the Now. That is precious indeed. The more you are focused on time—past and future—the more you miss the Now, the most precious thing there is." Life, as we know it, is a linear progression of events beginning at our birth and ending with our death. We look back into our past to relive our accomplishments or failures and look forward to ponder our future successes.

For us, time is a never-ending march forward; it never stops and is both impersonal and, seemingly, eternal. Henry David Thoreau stated, "The meeting of two eternities, the past and the future...is precisely the present moment." The NOW is the only place where one can actually experience and create. It is the only place where feelings exist. It is the only place where actions come to fruition. It is the only place where change happens. While you dream of the future and linger in the past, you live in the NOW. The future is nothing more than a preview of your creative process at work; the past is simply the results of past creative successes or failure.

> "Time is such a sublime realm, in which what you call past, present and future exist inter-relationally. That is, they are not opposites, but rather parts of the same whole; progressions of the same idea; cycles of the same energy; aspects of the same immutable Truth. If you conclude from this that past, present and future exist at one and the same 'time,' you are right."
>
> —Neal Donald Walsh

The Urantia Book states, "The time unit may be a day, a year, or a longer period, but inevitably it is the criterion by which the conscious self-evaluates the circumstances of life, and by which (man) measures and evaluates the facts of temporal existence." For us, time is, quite simply, the journey from our birth to our eventual demise, death. As we grow and mature through years, time is a linear progression of personal events and experiences. Time, it appears, has chosen our rise and our fall; it strips us of our youthful exuberance and replaces it with an aging perception of apathy. But what about the spiritual, does time exist in the realm of the eternal?

> "When the veil which now encloses us is no more, time will also be no more. Even now, time is clearly not our natural

dimension. Thus it is that we are never really at home in time. Alternately, we find ourselves impatiently wishing to hasten the passage of time or to hold back the dawn. We can do neither, of course. Whereas the bird is at home in the air, we are clearly not at home in time—because we belong to eternity! Time, as much as any one thing, whispers to us that we are strangers here. If time were natural to us, why is it that we have so many clocks and wear wristwatches?"

—Neal A. Maxwell

Thankfully time's journey ends when we die, or does it? It is only death, it is not the end of all existence, just the one we know. In fact, if time really does not exist, and it's a concept mankind has invented because he lacks the knowledge and understanding beyond this physical world, then death is not the terminator of life, as you would believe, but the terminator of time. Death squashes dreams of your future and erases your past while embracing you in an everlasting present.

How often have you looked through the window,
And seen the clear skies and valleys of peace?
Or heard the birds and the wind?
Or smelled the blossoms of spring while touching
Your love? You say you have done these
And more! All at once? Your side of the window
Offers this, its true, but then why do you search?
What are you searching for? You say for happiness
In the 'morrow. But it never arrives. You are trapped
In a world of todays, where every sunrise is followed
By a sunset, before you were and after you've been.
Each sense has its intimacy, its desire to be pleased.
But they are individuals, in search of one to lead.
Who will orchestrate their music? You search your past,
To prepare for your future. But you only live for today.

You must search for the rising sun in the Western skies.
There the senses play your melodious song. There,
The future does not rely on the past. Only today exists.
Forever!

As I approached the end of this section, I was surprised to find I formulated these concepts in a term paper many years ago while attending NYU in a middle-age history class taught by Professor Rutigliano. Somewhat startled, I straightened up as the last words of the section crossed the screen of my consciousness.

Tick, tock; tick, tock.

Chapter - 8

The Noumenon Called Love

*"Live love and you will live abundantly. Live love and
you will live joyously. Live love and you will live God.
Anything else is a rejection of who you are."*

—Spirit

There were no shadows. Shades of light created by sunshine peeking through outcrops of rocks and trees play an instrumental role in the life of a photographer. Without the stark variations of highlights and shadows, today's shoot would have to be enhanced in Photoshop or converted to compelling black and white.

When first laying eyes on the red sandstone formations marking the entrance of The Garden of the Gods, encompassing millions of years of geological history, I knew I had found a place of peace and solitude only nature could offer. To give the park its character, rocks, wildflowers and visually imposing gnarly juniper trees were placed in harmony in this public area located in the middle of Colorado Springs. The occasional deer, rabbits and birds completed the park's spiritual nature. Once one learns how to avoid the crowds, there are an abundance of places where one can sit in self-introspection and easily escape the overwhelming demands of society. I always make sure to visit the Siamese Twins, a structure forming a natural window with a direct, framed view of Pikes Peak. Garden of the Gods was the last place where I ever took a photo of Johnny. Sun flares, so pronounced in his pictures that day, were missing today.

The Siamese Twin Trail is a short half-mile loop appealing to many hikers who prefer an easier walk with stunning views in all directions. Waiting for people to clear the area, I was able to get the shot of a partially snow-capped Pikes Peak through the Twins' natural window. It reminded me of another photo I had taken of my son as he was looking through that very window with a huge smile and a backpack, almost as if he was preparing to enter another dimension. I didn't linger long. These days I rarely do.

Garden of the Gods has always been one of my favorite places to photograph or to just hike and breathe in the fresh, Colorado air. It never takes long to forget about problems of never-ending daily routines. My goal today was to find some appealing images of Cathedral Rock and Pikes Peak. These images would be added to my collection of a thousand pictures currently littering my computer's hard drive. Every now and then I browse through them always promising myself to make prints, then frame them and put them on display in some local restaurant or library. Lately, the enthusiasm needed to make this happen, was missing.

Cathedral Rock is a Garden of the Gods enigma. It's grey. Viewing it from the main parking lot, it looks like a large, unassuming hill of granite. From the other side, however, it appears majestic and significant. Best of all, this area of the park is rarely crowded and visited most often by people who search for more peaceful locations.

Backtracking Juniper Way Loop, I drove to the South Parking lot. Grabbing my camera I left Jannette reading her latest book and headed for Ridge Trail. Before me, Cathedral Rock dominated the surrounding red sandstone formations, while sunflowers provided a natural frame for the grey beauty as I snapped my first photograph. Taking several more pictures from various angles and perspectives, I continued along the uneven, rocky trail until Pikes Peak was fully visible. A lone figure was sitting on the very rock where, some years ago, I had taken a picture of Jannette meditating.

It was an area of the park where care needs to be taken when approaching the outcropping rocks facing Zebulon Pikes' discovery. Attempting to quietly circumnavigate the young lady, a loose rock gave way under my weight causing me to call out as I desperately tried to regain my balance while not dropping my Nikon D-700. She turned around to look at me.

"I'm so sorry for interrupting you, the rocks just gave out," I explained.

"That's OK. Are you alright?"

"I think so. This is one of my favorite places to shoot Pikes Peak."

"Mine too," she replied.

As she got up to leave, I noticed her green hat and its symbol. It looked familiar. "Excuse me, but your hat has a symbol very similar to a place I visited recently in Evergreen, called "All Things God.""

"That's where I got it from; my mom works there," she replied.

"Was meeting you here a moment of synchronicity," I wondered?

"James Redfield, *The Celestine Prophecy*, one of my favorite books," she replied.

"What does your mom do there?"

"Occasionally people come into the shop looking for readings. Were you planning on meditating here or just taking some pictures?"

"I was hoping to gain some further spiritual understanding, however it might appear," I replied.

"Like what?"

I wasn't prepared to open myself up emotionally, especially to a stranger. There was nothing about her, however, that would make me feel like she was insincere, and being familiar with the small Evergreen shop gave me more confidence in bringing up a subject I usually try to avoid. "I come here from time to time to remember my son."

"I'm sorry," she said, "I didn't realize."

"Not a problem."

We had reached a stage of awkward silence when she interrupted, "You know, he's in a better place?"

"I hear that all the time, but I have trouble understanding the afterlife."

"Not only does my mother do readings, but she also contacts souls who have transitioned, and she has told me about the reality and perception of love. She calls it the noumenon of love."

I wasn't sure if what this young lady had to say would be meaningful, but she apparently knew Malachi and in spite of my brief interaction with the man, I felt his sincerity and honesty. Besides, this was a moment of synchronicity which, I needed to let play out. "I'd be interested in hearing about this noumenon, or whatever."

Her eyes brightened and her smile exposed her dimples. "Love," she began to explain, "is probably the most misconstrued and misunderstood word in our society. It's being used as a noun, as a verb and even somehow portrayed as an adjective. If you were to ask ten people what their definition of love is, you may receive ten different answers; love is a feeling, love is a description, love is an action. Most of the time, however, we use the word love to describe our feelings for another person. It was Anonymous who probably described love in the best and most meaningful way possible:

'Love is patient; love is kind. It does not envy, it does not boast, it is not proud. It is not rude, it is not self-seeking, it is not easily angered, it keeps no record of wrongs. Love does not delight in evil but rejoices with the truth. It always protects, always trusts, always hopes, always perseveres.'

"Yet love is a universal embodiment of everything that is good, everything that is right with the world. 'Love conquers all,' as the saying goes, is the undeniable champion of all emotions and feelings. Through love we enter a dimension where evil, fear or any other transgressions are overcome; we enter a world of peace, joy and empathy. Per Gandhi, 'Where there is love there is life.'"

She opened her backpack and pulled out a piece of paper, "Here," she said, "read this, my mother wrote it."

I began to read.

> The time has come my friend
> For us to embrace,
> The time has come my friend
> To forgo this sad place.
> Our journey though brief
> Will take us afar
> Past mountains on high Beyond distant stars.
>
> Let our journey begin my friend,
> Examine your heart.
> Let our journey begin my friend,
> We won't stay apart.
> A new world lies ahead
> With green grass and blue skies,
> Painted with love and good will
> Unknown in our lives.
>
> Welcome my friend
> To an existence unknown,
> Welcome my friend
> To the seeds you have sown.
> Where democracy and law
> Don't exist high above,
> There are no concepts professed
> The noumenon is love.

"Very nice."

She continued to explain, love is anything one likes, anything encompassing goodness and those giddy, emotional feelings filling our bodies while clouding our judgment when a special someone arrives. Love, quite simply, defines everything good in this world and in our lives. But it is, most often, associated with a feeling and, therefore, is primarily defined as a sensation or emotion acting on us in a positive and endearing way. Love is the deepest and most vulnerable emotion known to man.

While this feeling of love can reach euphoric heights in an individual, it can never describe the love associated with God. Love, in the realm of the Divine, can never be a feeling or an emotion rising and falling according to the situation or relationship. Within God, love is an existence; it never varies and never falters. God is a state of love, impossible to replicate in our lives, yet God is more: God is Love!

Our big dichotomy: is love a feeling or an existence? Feelings diminish over time while love's existence is eternal. Death itself is not an end to all things; it's simply a transition from our physical state to the spiritual state of love. "Your son is there, believe me."

I tried to digest what this girl had relayed, unsure whether to believe it all or not. Doubt began to arise and a look of uncertainty was etched on my face. Before I could say anything she handed me a card, "Here, make an appointment with my mom. I'm sure she can help you come to terms with your loss." She smiled and walked away, "It was nice meeting you."

Lingering a while, I found several more photo opportunities and proceeded to snap a dozen or so pictures of Pikes Peak from various angles, when one final question entered my mind. I looked around, but she was gone. "Can I buy those hats at the store?" I yelled in the direction of an unsuspecting juniper.

After a few seconds I could hear the distant reply, "Yes!" Finding I was no longer absorbed in my photography I headed back to the car and Jannette.

"That was quick, what happened?"

"I met this girl..."

"You'd better be careful where you're going with this."

"Right, like I'm going to risk being a John Wayne Bobbitt."

"That's right! So what about this girl?"

"Her mom does readings at 'All Things God' and she thinks I should make an appointment to see if she can contact Johnny."

"Not a bad idea, you should do it."

I began to pull out of the parking lot and headed towards the exit. "Maybe I will."

"Good," she replied, "make sure you don't forget."

Driving northbound on I-25 I took the Monument exit. "Where are you going?"

"I want to take the back roads and stop off at the Sedalia Sanctuary."

"Any particular reason," she asked?

"Just need a place to reflect a bit."

"Let's go. You know I love walking the labyrinth."

It's always nice to take a scenic drive along secondary roads framed by ranches and open space. The ever-present foothills were closer and had more personality as crevices and outlying rock formations became more identifiable.

"This girl mentioned the noumenon called love. What do you think that meant?"

"Let me look up its meaning. How do you spell it? Never mind, I found it."

"What does it say?"

I waited awhile for Jannette's response as she began searching her phone for information. "It looks like it's a philosophy Immanuel Kant first devised meaning, simply the thing as it is as opposed to the thing observed."

"Hmm, wonder what that means?"

"It says here in Wikipedia that 'a noumenon is a posited object or event that exists independently of human sense and/or perception. The term noumenon is generally used in contrast with, or in relation to, the term phenomenon, which refers to any object of the senses.' Kinda like the difference between who we really are as opposed to how others see us."

"OK, so, I would think, one could apply it to other things besides people?" I reasoned.

"It would seem that way."

I continued, "She called it the noumenon of love. So the love we observe is different than what love actually is."

"Yes," Jannette interjected, "we see love as a personal feeling, one of the best feelings we can ever have. But that love doesn't compare to God's love, which isn't a feeling at all, but a state of being."

"I understand. We see love in our material world as something wonderful that excites our senses, like the giddy feeling I got when I first kissed you."

"You better still have that giddy feeling."

"Of course," I smiled, "you keep me giddy all day long." I stopped momentarily to recapture my train of thought. "So the noumenon is how we perceive love as opposed to living in a state of love. Our love is fleeting while God's love is permanent."

"So," Jannette began, "our love is with a lower case letter while God's love is with an upper case letter, love versus Love. The same word with a world of difference."

"Yes! One is a feeling and the other is being," I concluded.

We sat in silence reliving and analyzing the discussion we just had for the last few miles as we continued along Colorado Highway 105 until we reached Sedalia. When we reached the Sanctuary the sun was beginning to paint the sky red.

As usual, we were the only car in the parking lot. While Jannette headed for the labyrinth, I took a ribbon out of the trunk. This evening I would finally hang a foot-long banner on one of the six wishing trees at the Sanctuary Center. Its message was simple, "Johnny B" with a heart on either side. His final resting place might be in Pinelawn Cemetery on Long Island, but now his memory would forever dance in the Colorado winds. I could sense his smile. Taking a seat on the nearby bench, I sat in silence and watched the streamer tango in the wind along with hundreds of other well-wishing memories of multiple colors. One of the streamers with a Native American proverb caught my eye:

Listen to the wind,
It talks.
Listen to the silence,
 It speaks.
Listen to your heart,
It knows.

Wiping my eyes after saying a short prayer I headed down the stairs made of old, creosote treated railroad ties towards the labyrinth below knowing Johnny finally had a permanent foothold in a place dear to his heart, Colorado.

Laid out with large natural stones and surrounded by mature oak trees, I slowly followed the spiral path to the dominant altar rock at its center. I sat on an adjoining rock for a few minutes to reflect on the fragile nature of life and the purpose for our existence; but sometimes nothing seems to makes sense. Leaving the labyrinth took much less time than entering it as I realized events of the past could never be reversed. I began to hum and sing one of my favorite Beatles' songs, "Let It Be." It was McCartney who wrote the song after his mother, Mary, had passed and appeared to him in a dream. The catchy tune encouraged me to relax and take it easy. Even in the face of tragic loss, life goes on. "Let It Be" uplifted me as I began my walk back to the parking lot. Turning back once more and smiling broadly, I realized the labyrinth had done its job.

I reached the top of the stairs and, without looking back at the wishing trees, headed for the car where Jannette was waiting for me. We left the parking lot in silence as the sun dropped below the horizon leaving a large swath of red and yellow clouds hanging in the sky.

Chapter - 9

Brotherhood

*"Be of service to your fellow man and you will serve God.
Life is about giving, not receiving."*
—Spirit

*"One cannot proclaim the Fatherhood of God
while ignoring the brotherhood of man."*
—The Urantia Book

As I entered the classroom at the Academy of Lifelong Learning, Malachi was writing on the white board. It was a mathematical formula, "Brotherhood = Acceptance + Forgiveness." This was followed by the very well known Biblical phrase, "Love thy neighbor as thyself," with one small caveat, neighbor was lightly crossed out and above it he wrote brother.

"Hi," I said as I entered the room, "I guess today's class is about brotherhood."

"Based on what you see on the white board, I understand how you can surmise that but, in reality, today's class is really about ourselves. How we feel about ourselves is the precursor to how we feel about others. Once we understand and come to accept our Divine Oneness then our love for our fellow man is an automatic by-product. One cannot love their brothers unless one truly loves themselves."

"It's difficult to achieve in this world with all of the different ideals permeating this planet, different religions, different races, different eco-socio standards, different political views and so on and so on," I replied.

"Exactly! So how do we fight through all the obstacles to achieve unity? It's not about compromising our ideals to accept someone else's, but it's all about how we view ourselves and who we think we really are."

I noticed the chairs were placed in a circular fashion instead of the usual horseshoe shape and asked why the change.

"This way we can all see one another and no one is in the front or back. At God's table we are all equal," Malachi replied.

By the time he finished his reply, Sarah and Joanne were already seated with Mary and Paul following closely behind. "Good morning everyone," Malachi began, "today we're going to discuss brotherhood, what it means, how it evolves and why it's important. Does anyone care to take a stab at it?"

"Brotherhood is the elimination of personal biases and treating everyone as equal," Paul began.

"Good, anyone else?"

"Brotherhood is the total inclusion of all people into one globally united community," Joanne offered.

"Very good, anyone else?"

"To me it's simply an act of acceptance, not just allowing people to be different but also embracing their differences," Sarah offered.

"Isn't that critical," Malachi began, "how can we profess brotherhood when we don't embrace the differences within people? Are we not all different? We all think differently, act differently, look different, so why do we extrapolate differences due to race, politics and religion and judge those people to be unworthy of our acceptance? How often have we heard it said that my fellow Coloradoans are my brothers but not the Mexican immigrants residing here? What about Conservatives placing a negative label on Liberals, and vice versa? But before we can truly define brotherhood, where does it start, Hans?"

Hesitating a bit, I finally replied, "From within, where everything starts."

"OK, so you're saying it's more of an 'Innerhood' instead of a Brotherhood?"

It was Paul who rescued me, "Doesn't it depend on our definition of brotherhood? Is brotherhood an acceptance and recognition of equality with the people who share this planet with us, or is brotherhood that internal spiritual love we attribute to God?"

"You tell me," Malachi was quick to respond, "is there, or rather should there be a difference between the two?"

"I don't believe there should be a difference," Mary chimed in. "If we are truly children of God then there shouldn't be a difference at all. We are all equal in the eyes of God."

"There was a quote in *The Urantia Book*," I interjected to support Mary's claim, "One cannot proclaim the Fatherhood of God while ignoring the brotherhood of man."

"That sounds all well and good," Joanne said, "but it depends on who we think we are. If we're a physical species, then we are by nature judgmental and will continue to define brotherhood according to the filters of our value system. If we are spiritual beings immersed in the Love of God, then we cannot be anything but loving and accepting."

"Bravo!" Malachi let out a yell, smiling broadly, "You hit the nail on the head, Joanne and Hans, you were on the right track as well but you faltered in the stretch run. Everything starts with us and therefore the most important decision we can ever make is to determine who we really are. Are we physical beings spending a limited time on this planet only to return to the dust from whence we came? Or is our reality spiritual in nature owing our existence to the Love of God and, thereby, embracing every being as our brother in a realm, which knows no other way? Who believes our roots are derived from the spiritual nature of things?" Malachi stopped to survey the room, "Come on, raise your hands if you believe your true nature is spiritual rather than material."

Slowly I raised my hand and Sarah followed suit. It took another instant or so before Joanne and Mary raised their hands. Paul, I could see, was struggling with some internal issues before his hand went up, followed with a statement, "I believe I'm spiritual in nature, but I'm unsure how to apply that belief in my day-to-day life."

"That's OK."

"So, how do we get there?" Mary interrupted, as Malachi was about to enter into one of his lengthy explanations.

"By understanding who you really are!"

There was a moment of silence as, I suspect, everyone was thinking about who they really are and whether this scene before us, the classroom, the teacher and the students was real enough.

"What about forgiveness, how does that fit into all of this," Sarah asked, breaking the silence?

"That's an interesting question," Malachi began, "one would think brotherhood and forgiveness go hand in hand. But we have to be careful here. Too many people believe brotherhood and forgiveness do go hand in hand, and true brotherhood includes forgiving your brother for whatever you may not agree with. In this sense, we create a system of inequality. Having to forgive someone for whatever you don't agree with doesn't make him equal to you. Brotherhood is based on freedom! Each individual is free to choose his or her own life journey, unencumbered and, this is the kicker, without judgment. Forgiveness, more often than not, is self-imposed. All too often we feel the need to forgive someone when the actual need for forgiveness lies within ourselves. Brotherhood is more appropriately based on equality and acceptance of which forgiveness is a byproduct but not the main steering mechanism."

"So forgiveness doesn't play a role in brotherhood?" Paul interjected.

"I'm not saying it doesn't," Malachi began, "I'm saying forgiveness plays second fiddle to acceptance and equality. Not that forgiveness is not required, as you can see I've included it in our brotherhood formula, but it's not the primary focus. I see forgiveness of self playing a larger role than forgiving others."

"Why is that?" Paul asked.

"Forgiveness of others," Malachi continued, "is predominantly based on personal judgment, and judgment has no place when it comes to brotherhood. Embracing your fellow man in his endeavors and lending a hand whenever necessary is of primary importance. Don't judge what he's doing or how he's doing it. Brotherhood is about acceptance, not tolerance. There's a big difference here. Let your neighbor define who he is. Don't define him yourself, that's judgment. Remember, while forgiveness is important, the primary focus of forgiveness is directed on one self. You can only change yourself, not others. Everyone is different; there are no two people alike. You can see it by looking at your own household, your son, your daughter, your spouse, your relatives, your friends, etc., etc., etc. Accept their differences and their choices. Don't judge how they do it or why they do it; bless them, support them and wish them well. And always remember, God has no favorites; His love is unconditional regardless who you are or what you do."

"But what about sin? I asked. "

"Sin is self imposed judgment created by the absence of love in our material world. Remember, God is Unconditional Love and knows no sin. He sees us all through a loving light beholding everyone as perfect and complete. If there were any sin against God it would be our perception of separation, but even that cannot be true, regardless of our beliefs. So there are no sins against God. Sin was created in our world of form and was created by judgment and self-righteousness. Forgiveness of sins, therefore, is primarily an act of self-contrition which helps us to rid ourselves of guilt and fear."

"Then why does the church require the forgiveness of sins before one can be saved?" Mary asked.

"It's actually not required. We are already saved because we are one with God. Contrition and the resulting damnation or heavenly resurrection is a doctrine, which has been supported by the church body for hundreds of years. We can all guess why, but that will more likely than not take us too far off the subject at hand. Suffice it to say, we will all bask in the Love of God once our earthly time has come to an end. God's unconditional love will ensure everyone's salvation."

As the discussion continued I began to drift away from the class and enter my inner sanctum where questions and answers were comingled in one big serving of alphabet soup. I began to ponder the countless times I lowered my head in prayer and asked God to forgive me of my transgressions. Again and again, my need for forgiveness led me to pray in hopes of creating an inner peace devoid of fear. It seems living in this material world perpetuates sinful behavior again and again; whether it's judgment, jealousy, abuse, prejudice or a host of other transgressions. It seems sin is an inherent presence in our society.

With sin, as I was taught, comes forgiveness. Prayers of forgiveness, I reasoned, must flow heavenward at an alarming rate, judging by what is currently transpiring in this day and age. Not only do we seek God's forgiveness but also from others whom we have mistreated in one way or another.

But does God forgive our every transgression? Is He so preoccupied with our behavior that every vain thought or misdeed requires heavenly intervention? I don't think so. I agree with Malachi when he declared that in the eyes of God there is only one transgression requiring forgiveness and it's our belief in separation. Separating ourselves from God is the ultimate sin and one He has already forgiven us for. Since all other sins stem from our belief of separation, it is only the belief in separation, which requires God's forgiveness. While all of this may make sense, God is always fully aware of the Universal Oneness and as such doesn't need to forgive us for anything. He knows we are all united in a Universal Whole and as such are perfect and complete. There is no need to forgive for Love knows only Love.

As for the rest of our transgressions, they are created by us and, therefore, require our forgiveness, not God's. However, for us to truly forgive, we need to forgive ourselves first, for how can we forgive others if we can't forgive ourselves?

We must understand that once we accept our separation from God, His love and peace and joy are replaced with fear, uncertainty and judgment. Our sins against man are those deeds and thoughts we have against one another. Our sin against God is rejecting the Oneness. Once we realize our misconception and accept our true selves, all transgressions against one another will disappear for Love begets Love, it knows no sin.

I could envision Malachi's additional message, "Our failure to acknowledge The Oneness has created the great God dichotomy. This dichotomy is not an attribute of God but caused by our rejection of Him. Too many of us see God as outside ourselves and those who understand He exists within us have trouble grasping this fact because of the turmoil and demands of the world around us. We fail to understand, once we embrace and return to whence we came, the Oneness, all else doesn't matter. Embracing the Love of God is all we need to do and everything will be provided for us."

Malachi's powerful message and insight led me to my internal library of events long since passed to a time when I was languishing in a sea of malaise filled with discarded dogmas, a time I struggled with my spirituality. Struggling was an acceptable way of saying I didn't care about spirituality or any of its tenets. Making a living and surviving in this world in the most comfortable way possible was at the forefront of my mind. Juggling professional demands and the responsibilities required to raise children was all I could handle. God and prayer were the last options to problems seemingly too large to bear. Prayers were never answered and God seemed to be a distant, non-caring deity whose religious representatives cared more about building the church body than helping with my particular hardships. My family was my priority and nothing else really mattered. All my energy was focused on personal issues; there was no time to worry about anyone else.

My concerns centered on my world. How could I care about others when I could barely take care of myself? It became easy to plummet into a regimen, which included only work and home. Expanding beyond my tight little circle of acquaintances was not anything I explored or desired. I built my own little prison and felt safe in its confining principles. The kids certainly didn't mind and I found solace in playing with them. My life of single-mindedness felt comfortable and provided a sense of stability; I created my paradigm and felt content behind its four walls.

It seems to me much has been made of equality by race, gender, religion, sexual persuasion and politics. Yet, by categorizing these qualities we are more apt to separate the populace than to unite them. Brotherhood is a condition of society whereby all men are considered equal and free to pursue their lives however they wish without infringing on anyone else. It is also a circumstance whereby all men share empathy for one another and offer help and support whenever needed. Quite simply, brotherhood is the love for our fellow man.

Perhaps no other human condition has been more abused or misunderstood. History has shown circles of brotherhood are often predetermined and limited to a select few. There are all types of brotherhoods, Catholics, Muslims, Germans, gays, senior citizens, etc., they are mostly predicated on belief or geography or economics. Brotherhoods have become an idealistic union of individuals based on common precepts. But these unions are micro-brotherhoods who fail or refuse to understand the broader principles behind the ideal. These micro groups serve more to divide instead of bonding. True brotherhood is an all-encompassing acceptance of every person, not just a select few. It is an ideal fostered by the sages and prophets from ancient times to this modern era. "If anyone says, 'I love God,' and hates his brother, he is a liar; for he who does not love his brother whom he has seen cannot love God whom he has not seen" (John 4:20).

Today's climate of political nationalism is creating a deeper chasm amongst ethnic, religious and political groups worldwide. The nationalist is more concerned with the well being within his own state instead of others outside of it, often leading to discriminatory principles. Morals, beliefs and judgments are based on precepts which, more often than not, are forced on a minority whose beliefs are not always aligned with the majority. Usurping power and deep biases are distressing by-products of such a society.

Christian ideals, while often used to rationalize such nationalistic principles, don't advocate such behavior. Jesus, himself was a tolerant man with an all-inclusive mindset welcoming all into his inner circle. "There is neither Jew nor Gentile, neither slave nor free, nor is there male and female, for you are all one in Christ Jesus" (Galations 3:28).

The moment one places an adjective before the word brotherhood, it diminishes the broad spectrum of its meaning, limiting its scope and universal intent. In its macro sense, brotherhood encompasses the universal body of man, regardless of race, gender, age or any other divisive systematic categorization. In addition, it incorporates those inherent rights and freedoms given to all men, which cannot be arbitrarily curtailed. "For to be free is not merely to cast off one's chains, but to live in a way that respects and enhances the freedom of others" (Nelson Mandela).

"Have we not all one Father? Hath not one God created us? There is 'one mind common to all individual men.' It is impossible to depart from this Divine Presence, to be separated from this heavenly Father. Since God is everywhere, wherever we are God is.

Today I know that there is one Spirit in everyone I meet. Realizing that there is one Heavenly Father, I know that there is a brotherhood of humanity. There are no aliens, no strange persons. The Divine Image in me cannot be separated from the Divine Image in others. I see God in everyone I meet and the Spirit that is within me responds to the Spirit within them, for we have one Father."

—Ernest Holmes

We are not brothers because we walk upright on two legs or because we share beliefs in the same politics or dogmas, we are brothers because we are all creations of the same God. We all share the same heritage and have the same internal God center connecting us to Divine

Energy. What we continually fail to realize is whatever we do affects us all. Once mankind begins to realize its interdependency on all living beings, then one can begin to forge a true bond of brotherhood with all men. As long as judgment and biases against other men remain, brotherhood will always be a pipe dream away. In today's world, religions often expounding on the benefits of brotherhood, more often serve to isolate one sect from another, thereby destroying the very message it professes.

True brotherhood will never exclude anyone. It is always open to all and will always accept different beliefs and ideals. Brotherhood proudly accepts diversity without judgment and discrimination. Michael Jackson and Lionel Richie captured this ideal perfectly in their song "We Are the World," recorded to raise money for hunger relief in Africa. Their Live Aid Concert raised awareness that hunger was very real and should not exist in our modern society. It advanced the call for universal brotherhood crossing political, religious and racial boundaries. This world-wide event, featuring many renowned artists, fostered an outpour of brotherhood rarely seen before.

Looking up, I was sure the smiling face of Malachi was pleased with my assessment as my favorite passage from the Urantia book emerged in my mind, "One cannot proclaim the Fatherhood of God while ignoring the brotherhood of man." A new formula became apparent in my mind, "Brotherhood = Acceptance." Malachi was right; forgiveness of others has nothing to do with the circle of Universal Brotherhood.

Chapter - 10

Experiencing the Light

*"Embrace not the ways of the world,
but rather embrace the return to Spirit.'*
—Spirit

Her soft voice beckons me
To follow her.
Unhesitatingly I raise my spirit,
And I am gone.
I find myself adrift
Towards that wonderful light.

I am in darkness,
Surrounded by light. I am in a void,
Surrounded by emotions. I am dead,
Surrounded by life.

Life is life
And death is death,
If I must choose one,
I will have no breath.
I am in a euphoria,
Of which I have never known.
I am surrounded by warmth,

Of which I have never known.
I am beckoned onward,
To which I have never known.
Death is death
And life is life, In my new world
I will know no strife.

I think of my family,
Who are they?
I think of my friends,
Where are they?
I think of the Divine,
What are they?

Life is the beginning.
Death is the end.
Death is the beginning!
There is no end!

Malachi's classes reignited my urge to begin meditating, and again a meditative message came to me: Death is a simple, painless transition from form to spirit. It is like taking off our clothes and being in true form, true spirit. It is here where we can experience God's love. God's love is a high vibration enveloping all there is. This vibration passes through our bodies like radio waves pass through us unknowingly. Our form vibrates too slowly for us to pick up the high vibrations of God's love. Only the enlightened have been able to do so.

As we die, we enter the world of spirit at a higher vibration level. Here we become aware of God's love vibration. God's love vibration is pure; it can be nothing else. This is why God is not jealous, judging or punishing. These human qualities are unable to exist in a state of pure love. Death is our doorway to this pure love. There is not one atom in God that is less than pure, for it would make God impure and that is something He could never be. How do we know this? God awakens us in mysterious ways.

My past meditations were completely different than this one. Normally I would internally travel to different places with some spiritual significance, but this was different. It was a message for me about death. Was I being prepared for an earlier than normal exit from this world? Was it a message to get my personal life in order? One thing I was sure about, this would manifest itself fairly quickly.

I didn't have to wait long. Two days later I had the experience of a lifetime. For me it happened in what I can only describe as a near death experience, except I wasn't sick or injured or overly stressed; I was sleeping peacefully.

My brief journey into this spiritual universe began with a soft, feminine voice calmly whispering to me as I slept, telepathically requesting that I arise, "Hans, get up, you're dead, we have to go." I saw myself sitting up in bed thinking I was going to praise God and see my dear deceased friends Patsy and Johnny. One final "We have to go," and I found myself longing to merge with the Light.

Initially I saw myself sleeping next to my first wife, Lynn, before I began floating easily towards the Light, mesmerized by an indescribable sensation of euphoria. I did not think about my family who I was leaving behind. The physical world, with all of its problems, concerns and worries, was not an issue here. No adversary or ill feeling could possibly pierce this armor of joy and happiness. Here tranquility, peace and love abounded. The Light called me and I was more than willing to merge with it. I was completely immersed in the NOW and the Love surrounding me.

I could see myself, in what appeared to be a long, white flowing gown, drifting effortlessly towards the Light. This wonderful Light appeared like the rising sun, emanating brilliantly tapered illuminations from its sides until they blended with their horizon. This Light radiated warmth, which enveloped my entire being, while illuminating the horizon with unequaled, yet non-blinding, brightness. Above all, this radiance propagated an unparalleled sensation of love.

It was the most beautiful thing I have ever experienced; the warmth, the love, the peace, the joy and the knowing, a knowing this is where I wanted to be. Nothing else mattered! The Light called with an unparalleled brightness, which would have been blinding in my physical world. This Light was multi-dimensional, it had warmth and feeling, it exuded peace and love; it was the first time I felt true Love. It wasn't only a feeling, it was a being; my soul had emerged from its lifelong hibernation to introduce me to my True Self. I finally knew what it was like to be immersed in Divine Oneness. I was coming home! Not only did I see the Light and myself, I was being the Light and myself! All my senses were activated to their extreme euphoria. All my doubts and fears of physical death were erased. All the love I could possibly bear filled me to a point of bursting and not one iota of judgment remained in my consciousness. It was love and purity in its highest form. I was no longer my physical self, I had reawakened to my spiritual self; I had returned to who I really was.

As I was floating towards this bright aurora, I found myself wanting to see my feet. This was followed by another telepathic message saying it was not yet my time. This conscious connection to the physical dimension was, I believe, what prompted my return. Why my feet? I will never know. Perhaps, after carrying me for all of these years, they felt abandoned, useless as I was floating in air. In any case, a gentle tap on my shoulder awoke me and I found myself sitting up in my bed thinking, "WOW! I was just dead." However, the tremendous sensation of love was still within me, a feeling unequaled in our physical world, an emotion so great I wanted to immediately return to my newly discovered dimension.

While emotions in our physical space can turn in an instant, this euphoria of Love would not leave me. It diminished over time and took several days to fully dissipate. Try as best as I could, this Love would not stay. From this moment on, existing in a world where peace and love were continuously overwhelmed by differences and conflict would be difficult. God had given me the gift of experiencing His Love. I'm sure it was just a small sample, as I believe our physical selves could never embrace the fullness of His being; it would put us on an emotional overload.

I have heard many recorded instances of people spiritually floating towards a Light. The Light and an unequaled feeling of love are some of the characteristics near death encounters have in common. Some have only viewed the Light, while others have actually entered it. Some have met deceased parents and friends, while others have met God. All have, however, for a variety of reasons, returned to their physical environments with a renewed outlook on life and, most importantly, death. The Light, how do we get there? What is it?

It took me back to a time my father was under Hospice care. Under the influence of morphine to ease the pain of his bone cancer, he would drift off for hours, awakening with an enlightened face while recounting his travels to beautiful gardens where he met his parents and siblings welcoming him home. He affirmed his fear of death had been overcome to the point where he was thankful for leaving his stricken body behind. He began to look forward to returning to his spiritual home where peace and love awaited him. It was not only an acceptance of the inevitable, he was looking forward to it! For him, the dichotomy between the physical and spiritual had been resolved. The reality of things finally became clear beyond all doubt as he embraced the realm of Spirit: true and everlasting Love exists, he assured us, beyond this earthly world.

To understand the Light, one must, perhaps, comprehend death. Is death, as many perceive, the termination of life, or, as others believe, the gateway leading to the genesis of a new existence? Robert Lifton, in his book *Living and Dying* states, "Death is simply a fact - the inevitable end of biological life." It is the point of time when the heart stops beating or the brain ceases to function. As such, nearly 160,000 people die on this earth every day, over 5,000 in the United States alone. The inevitable truth is all living organisms, plants and animals alike, must die.

Suddenly a vision of Teacher entered my consciousness. Death he stated is the gateway to our spiritual domain, the place where we all belong. It is, perhaps, the greatest fear of all mankind because it threatens to terminate our individual existence forever. He explained how some doctors, philosophers and scientists viewed death.

He began with Elisabeth Kubler-Ross whose *On Death and Dying* defines five stages of death. The first stage, denial and isolation, is the belief one's imminent death cannot be near, and, therefore, becomes an attempt to come to terms with its revelation.

Anger, the next stage, ignites a resentment of family, friends and even God that life will end prematurely. Bargaining, the third stage is an attempt to compromise with God to delay the inevitable. Depression sets in with the realization when one's demise cannot be reversed, cannot be compromised. The final stage, acceptance, is, perhaps, the most noteworthy. At this stage one actually prepares himself to die, and generally wishes to be left alone and not be interrupted by outside events. My father, I realized, had reached this stage as he had overcome his fear of death.

Kubler-Ross questions why someone who has fought to prevent his ultimate fate, should resign himself, as the last stage suggests, to accept it? Could they, at this stage, be aware of another dimension, another universe awaiting them? Death may be viewed as the curtain, or veil, between the existence we are conscious of and one hidden from us. Have these individuals, who are so near death, witnessed a phenomena that fortifies and strengthens their souls, thereby allowing them to readily accept their fate? Have they seen the Light? While these questions continue to be asked by medical personnel worldwide, a few of us have actually experienced the post-death phenomena.

Next he cited Melvin Morse, MD who states, "Those that experience the Light say that it is more than just light. There is a substance to it that 'wraps' them in a warmth and caring that they have never before felt." Morse has been studying patients who have had near-death experiences, events that have brought them close to clinical death. These patients, after recovering from their illnesses, have related astonishing tales of spiritual encounters. Some have spoken to friends, while others have spoken with God. But all have seen the Light, have

felt the Light, and have, forever more, been profoundly affected by it.
Teacher then referenced Phyllis Zauner, in her book *Puzzling Visions
of the Near- Dead*, who relays what many people have experienced:

"Soon after you realize you are dead, you hear ringing or
buzzing noises, and you are hurtled through a long, dark
tunnel. After this, you find yourself out of your own body,
floating above the scene you've just been part of.

Detached and interested, you watch the resuscitation attempt
on your body. You are greeted by friends and relatives who
have already died reaching out to help you. Then a loving
spirit of a kind you have never encountered, bathed in dazzling
light, appears and non-verbally asks you to evaluate your life,
helping you along by playing back scenes of major events."

Teacher went on to explain this Light is not a light at all, at least
not the way we understand it. It is a multi-dimensional being with
intelligence and feeling vastly superior to anything existing in our
physical state. It is a spiritual radiation of intense compassion far
transcending our current comprehension. This bright Illumination is
the omnipotence, omnipresence and omniscience of the God many
people worship. Quite simply, this Light is love; God is love.

It is, therefore, understandable why people who have had near-death
experiences remember them so vividly. These events often change a
person's complete outlook and reaction to life. They now understand
a vastly superior existence awaits them, one they yearn to return to.
Zauner goes on to explains how patients reacted after having a near
death experience:

"...They were left with the feeling there was a purpose
connected with the experience, that it was an experience of
lasting benefit that it was a spiritual experience, and that life
had been changed by the experience."

I realized the commonality of most of those who have had near-death experiences is the remembrance and effect of the Light. It is not an inanimate object, a source of electricity or energy, as we know light to be, but it is, instead, alive with all of the wonderful feelings one can hope for. It is this "being" which sets this voyage apart from any other. But for those who have entered it, it becomes another universe alive with magnificent scenery and friendly and loving spirits and, of course the Supreme Being from whence all things radiate. Wilson reports, "Having entered the light, the resuscitated now report finding themselves in extraordinarily beautiful surroundings that are unequivocally stereotypes of popular concepts of heaven."

Wilson goes on to explain all of the senses appear to have a heightened awareness making the journey so much more powerful. "There were many people all dressed in glowing white robes with radiant faces. They looked beautiful. The air smelled so fresh. I have never smelled anything like it." Communication is, in many cases telepathically transmitted. It is not necessary to speak, although one can if he so desires, but thoughts are transmitted readily and are clearly understood. There is no need to interpret what was said or meant. "...Telepathic means of communication recurs repeatedly though by no means universally in the description of near-death experiencers' meetings with the deceased."

Teacher continued, "When one speaks of a spiritual world, one cannot ignore the beliefs of the many religions around the world preaching the existence of a god and a place of eternal happiness. While their foundations and doctrines differ greatly, they share that commonality of a spiritual universe providing peace and everlasting tranquility. Can the millions of Christians, Muslims and Buddhists be wrong? Is there not, instilled deep within us, a hint or feeling that something greater than us does exist in some form or universe? We cannot possibly investigate all of the possible religious connotations near- death experiences provide. It will only stress the similarity of the near-death journey and the inherent belief of millions of religious followers that a spiritual being and existence should be worshipped and eulogized.

"Yet," Teacher assured, "nothing instills more fear than the fear of death; while nothing raises the curiosity more than the possible existence or life after death. When the soul returns to the Oneness, it sheds its illusionary material coat and returns to the state of grace from which it came. Grace, like Love and Enlightenment, is a state of Being; it's not a feeling. We all exist in a constant State of Grace, both in the material and spiritual domains. It is the ego or attachment to the objective world that keeps us from this realization. Letting go of your attachments will awaken you to your spirituality. Most people are reluctant to do this hence, death is the assurance we will all find our way home to the Oneness.

"Your purpose here is not to accumulate wealth or notoriety, but simply to awaken. By awakening to your spiritual roots, you will inherently build a society where the oneness of mankind exists. This is true brotherhood. Imagine a subjective Spiritual Oneness and an objective material oneness encompassing all the universes. As Spiritual Oneness and material oneness merge, the ego disappears and death is no longer necessary. Everything is whole and complete!

"I'm sure some of this has left you confused," Teacher rationalized as his vision slowly faded from my consciousness, "but I felt this was an important enough subject to investigate from several points of view. Most of these perspectives confuse and cloud what death is in actuality. Death, quite simply is a gateway between the physical and spiritual realm. It is a time when we discard our illusion of separation and embrace the multi-dimensional world of spirituality. It is a time when we return to who we really are."

"What about judgment," I asked?

"There is no judgment! There is no forgiveness! God is Unconditional Love! Judgment and forgiveness exist in our world and provide a need for us to feel better about ourselves. God has no need to forgive anyone for he knows we are spiritual in nature, He knows we exist within the Oneness and, as such, we are eternal and loving. God will never forsake us and cast us to the fires of hell. Hell is nothing more than our belief in separation, our perceived time separated from the Oneness. For every instant we see ourselves as separated from God is an instant we spend in our self-imposed hell."

"So there is no secret to being saved," I asked?

"No," Teacher whispered, "we are all children of God regardless of our belief. Heaven awaits us all. You can call on me anytime." And as quickly as he had appeared, he was gone.

With my out of body experience still fresh in my mind, I finally understood the gates of heaven reside within every one of us. More importantly, I was fortunate enough to have received a glimpse of what lay behind those gates. What about Johnny? According to Teacher's message he was basking in spiritual bliss. I had to find out.

Chapter - 11

Opportunity Cost

"Events are the occurrences which lay the groundwork
for your life experience."
—Spirit

"The universe is infinite and it seeks to expand through the
consciousness of every individual upon the face of the earth."
—Frank Richelieu

The car ride was unusually quiet. For me it was another time of introspection, a time when thoughts emerged in my mind and stayed there until they were recognized and addressed. These days they popped up more often than not and I realized my antiquated view of spirituality was on the verge of collapse. My old view embracing God somewhere out there, outside of me was being seriously challenged, while the new age message of God being within was beginning to make more and more sense to me.

Entering the house I took my customary seat on the den sofa.

"You're awfully quiet," Jannette began, "what's up?"

"Just thinking about things."

"What kind of things?"

I thought about this question a bit and wasn't sure if this was the time to begin an in depth discussion of my mental conflict between God and man. "God," I replied.

She gave me the usual cross-eyed look when she realized I was at a crossroad of some type. "Want to talk about it?"

"It might help."

"OK, let's have it."

"Well, ever since I began the course at the Academy and met the instructor."

"Malachi?"

"Yes, ever since I met him I've been trying to understand these spiritual and material concepts and how they affect me."

"You mean how do you explain you're spiritual in nature living in a material world?" Jannette asked.

"I guess that's one way of putting it." I waited a bit to collect my thoughts and continued, "I have difficulty coming to terms with the concept we are all one with God. It began when Malachi attempted to clarify omnipresence, omniscience and omnipotence for me. Once I came to understand omnipresence, the others kinda fell in place. He also helped me understand consciousness and gave me a clearer insight into the cycle of creation. Then the girl at Garden of the Gods mentioned the state of love and hinted of an afterlife. Finally, his messages of brotherhood and death. It's a lot to digest for a rational mind."

"Rational? You're the craziest person I know."

I smiled. "Sometimes, but I do have my lucid moments. How do you put it all together, especially when I include the experience of the Light?"

Jannette tilted her head sideways as her eyes circled upwards, "Faith! I try not to get too deep. I just know there's a God and we're all included in His Oneness. This God is not the one I learned about in Catholic school; He's not a judge or protector. God is a creator and so are we; He experiences through us."

"I get that," I replied, "but how do you tap into His energy so I can learn to let go of these material desires. I get the feeling life is one big lesson of opportunity cost."

"Yes," she laughed, "Professor Lerner, that's the only thing I learned in his Economics class at NYU."

I began to drift into my daydream, or was my internal Teacher connection raising its voice again? Quite simply, it began, opportunity cost is the endeavor not chosen when making a decision. Every decision has the potential for several outcomes, some more favorable than others. Unfortunately, the consequences of each decision may not become apparent until long after the decision has been made. It's the reason why decision-making is a process not to be taken lightly. Fortunately, we always have the power and means to change and reverse course. It's what I call the cha-cha of life, two steps forward and one step back.

Suppose you are walking in the woods looking for berries and you come upon a fork in the trail. Right or left is a relatively easy decision to make, but after you make it, the consequences of that decision do not always become apparent. In some cases you will never know. Let's say, you decide to take the right path and a half mile later you run upon a host of bushes brandishing the most beautiful, delicious looking berries. Picking until your basket is full you head home content and happy.

When reaching that initial fork in the road you run into a hiker coming from the left fork. He is carrying two baskets of berries. He tells you about the abundance of berry bushes a hundred yards down the road, just over the small ridge. There are so many berries he proclaims I can't carry them all.

While your initial choice worked out well for you, as you garnish a basket full of wonderful berries, taking the left fork seems to have been a better choice. Not only were there more berries, but you lost precious time walking the half mile down the right fork, time that could have been used gathering more berries only a hundred yards away down the left fork. You're now left wondering what might have been and question your decision.

Opportunity cost raises its specter for every decision; do I do this or that and what do I sacrifice? A series of bad decisions can, therefore, be quite costly. So how do you maximize your decision making process? Bring in a wild card; bring in Spirit. Spirit will never lead you astray; Spirit will never throw you a curve ball. Spirit only knows Truth and Love. There's never an opportunity cost with Spirit, only an opportunity lost.

Going back to that fork in the road while opening your heart to Spirit, whichever direction presents itself in your consciousness, is the right one. If you take the left fork you find berries in abundance only a hundred yard away. If Spirit sends you towards the right fork, you still find the berries you are seeking, but Spirit may have prevented you from tripping and falling going along the other fork. There will never be doubt lingering in your mind if you decide to follow Spirit. A collateral bonus is your acceptance of Spirit and an increasing faith helping you to strengthen an internal trust and bond with your inner self. Self-introspection is a powerful tool presenting opportunities and choices from a perspective of love, which always has our best interest in mind.

More important is judgment. Constant judgment of people or events cause us to lose sight of our spiritual connectedness while accentuating our separateness. Once we give in to this judgment, we enter a whole new world where differences not only exist, but are scrutinized and bastardized. As a result we become locked into our physical perception of reality; we move further away from the loving kindness existing within us all. Acceptance and rejection are two diametrically opposed principles and whichever one we choose will lead us down a different road of possibilities and experience.

Here then is the first life changing decision to be made. Do you follow the less traveled road of Spirit or the well-worn path of human ego? One road will, most likely, offer a quick return on your decision whose rewards will be much more fleeting, while the other road will offer you long term security and, quite possibly, more lasting riches. Granted they will both lead back to Spiritual Oneness, but one path is filled with struggles and conflict while the other is filled with possibilities of personal and civic growth and unity. Looking at these options, one also realizes both lead to the exact same destination, which is eternal love, peace and joy. There are no exceptions. Our

Oneness with the Divine will not allow it; fortunately, it's just a matter of time before we all awaken to the Truth.

Annie Hutton in her article "Spiritual Opportunity" states the cost of ignoring Spirit. "This means that the opportunity cost we have forgone is the Spiritual Path where we make time to just 'BE', let go of ego, serve God and each other, and generally glide through this life with ease and grace. Now in what Universe would this be considered the 'second best choice'??!!"

By choosing Spirit, Annie says you can never go wrong. There is never a wrong choice when selecting the path of Spirit; hence, there will never be an opportunity cost, only an opportunity lost. This lost opportunity presents itself when Spirit becomes the alternate choice, not the primary one.

With Spirit all things are possible. In his *Spiritual Economics* book, Eric Butterworth states the following:

A person who keeps conscious that the divine flow is ever centered within one has faith that limitless substance will find expression through him or her in the form of creative ideas, ingenuity, the will to work, and a security of work opportunities. It could be said that when you realize your relationship to the dynamic Universe (Spirit), you are forever in a field where you can drill for oil and bring in a gusher every time.

In his Sermon on the Mount, Jesus told his followers:

"Do not lay up for yourselves treasures on earth, where moth and rust consume and where thieves break in and steal, but lay up for yourselves treasures in heaven, where neither moth nor rust consumes and where thieves do not break in and steal. For where your treasure is, there will your heart be also."

(Matthew 6:19-21)

Opportunity cost, it must be remembered, is never a spiritual phenomenon, only a human one. Choosing Spirit, regardless of the choice made, can never have any adverse consequence; it can only be a choice that's filled with Truth, Joy, Peace and Love. Spirit knows no other way. Remember, Spirit doesn't give you the choice of heaven or hell, for hell is any place where Spirit is not. But the good news is Spirit is everywhere and it is only our awareness of it that's lacking. Butterworth goes on to say: "So you give thanks, not for these things, but from the awareness that there is always an all-sufficiency even within the insufficiency."

All it takes is faith. Faith has quite often been misconstrued as a firm belief something will come to pass. First and foremost, Faith is not and never has been a belief, whether it's in something or that something will happen. In this sense, prepare to be disappointed. Faith is a knowing! It is knowing something will come to pass, and, in this sense, it can only happen through Spirit. But knowing something will come to pass also requires the recognition when it presents itself. Financial abundance doesn't necessarily show up as a million dollar check in the mailbox. It presents itself as an opportunity for a promotion or a request for your services. Opportunities abound when a heart filled with Spirit is grounded in Faith.

Whether knowingly or unknowingly, we make decisions constantly, many of them are responded to automatically and don't take a lot of effort to rationalize. But many decisions take time and effort and often lead us on a path of anxiety and confrontation. Spirit will never guide us in those directions. On the Dharma Wheel web site exists the following quote by Luke on its "Opportunity Cost as a Spiritual Concept" thread: "The opportunity cost of wasting a moment on something trivial, is the meaningful spiritual activity we could have been doing at that moment."

Teacher continued with a Native American insight. "There are many roads in life, but there are two that are important; the Red Road and the Black Road. They represent good and bad in every one's life. They are the two choices people have to make frequently in life. The Red

Road is the good way, the good side, and the right choice. It is a road that is difficult, with dangers and obstacles that are hard to travel on. The Black Road is the bad way, the bad side, and the wrong choice. The Black Road is wide and easy to travel. The Red Road and the Black Road appear in our lives not as roads but as the personifications of right and wrong, good and bad, light and dark."

> Our quest, our earth walk, is to look within,
> to know who we are,
> to see that we are connected to all things,
> that there is no separation,
> only in the mind.
>
> —Lakota Seer

Jannette interrupted my daydream, "Hey, where are you?"

"Oh, sorry. I was just delving a bit deeper about opportunity cost. I'm also tempted to meet Hannah and see if she can contact Johnny."

"That's not a bad idea. Maybe your mom and dad will come through as well," Jannette replied. "It's time you come to terms with your losses. Trust Spirit and take the shot."

I reached for the phone and dialed. "Hello Malachi?"

It seemed almost as if he was expecting my call, "Yes, Hans, hello."

"I'd like to schedule a session with Hannah."

"Why, of course, I'll set it up for you."

Chapter - 12

Valley of Sunflowers

*"Do not allow the magnitude of the infinity, the immensity of the
eternity, and the grandeur and glory of the matchless character of
God to overawe, stagger, or discourage you; for the Father is not
very far from any of you; he dwells within you, and in him do we all
literally move, actually live, and veritably have our being."*
—The Urantia Book

It seems there are always more questions than answers as the thirst
for knowledge drives us ever forward to find those new horizons
created in our minds. Thinking is an automatic process as each passing
moment creates new experiences impacting our lives.

As I enter the twilight of my tenure in this physical realm, I am still
not entirely sure how our material world is impacted by the spiritual
realm.

No one, it appears, has a firm grasp on the exact connection we
have with God. All too often we are reminded of a God who watches
over his realm dispersing favors and forgiveness to those who profess
a certain belief or whose behavior follows a certain norm. Everywhere
you look, God is defined in material terms. Attempting to define God
in human terms is akin to attempting to fit a square peg into a circular
hole. God is not a physical being, and with all the difficulties this
human experience brings, why would He want to be?

Conforming to the ways of the material world pleases no one but those who exist therein. Rules for governing, worshipping, justice, economy, communication, travel, etc., etc. were established here on this earthly plane, not by any deity, but by mankind. Included in these expectancies are the rules of engagement between individuals and their established societies. This is a world of individuals competing for similar resources in order to survive. Rather than working in harmony, mankind has established a competitive system based primarily on Darwin's vision of evolution; people are in competition for their own survival. This vision only serves to further separate and divide.

This vision not only chains us more to the material environment, it also serves to establish special interest factions searching for resources for personal gain. Their mantra becomes, therefore, "me first and everyone else be damned." God, as is often taught, looks after his own flock, those who worship and bestow tribute unto Him. His personal clergy have become the intermediaries who dispense his message to individuals outside of their dogmatic inner circle.

However, Malachi's message portrays a totally different deity with a structure at complete odds with the consensus of our material existence. God is not an individual being; He is an all-inclusive spirit embellishing more the principles professed by Ernest Holmes:

1. God is the Living Spirit Almighty, one, indestructible, absolute, and self-existent Cause. This One manifests itself in and through all creation but is not absorbed by its creation. The manifest universe is the body of God; it is the logical and necessary outcome of the infinite self-knowingness of God.

2. God is the incarnation of the Spirit in everyone and that all people are incarnations of the One Spirit.

3. He is the eternality, the immortality, and the continuality of the individual soul, forever and ever expanding.

4. Heaven is within us and that we experience it to the degree that we become conscious of it.

5. He professes the ultimate goal of life to be a complete

emancipation from all discord of every nature and that this goal is sure to be attained by all.

6. He claims the unity of all life and that the highest God and the innermost God is one God.

7. That God is personal to all who feel this indwelling Presence.

8. God is the direct revelation of Truth through the intuitive and spiritual nature of the individual and that any person who lives in close contact with the indwelling God may become a revealer of Truth.

9. The Universal Spirit, which is God, operates through a Universal Mind, which is Law of God and that we are surrounded by this creative Mind, which receives the direct impress of our thought and acts upon it.

10. We create our environment and existence through the power of this Mind.

11. God is eternal Goodness, the eternal Loving-kindness, and the eternal Creator of Life to all.

12. God exists in our own soul, our own spirit, and our own destiny, for we understand that the life of all is God.

But what is the connection between God and man? After all, we exist in this physical world attempting to build a better environment for our children hoping they don't make the same mistakes we made. By and large, everything we teach our children is a course of survival focused on our material world. Non-tangible things are easily dismissed as irrelevant unless the wind blows too hard or the temperature gets too hot or cold. As a results based society even thinking is often dismissed as silly unless there are tangible results. Quite simply, our existence is physical and our lives are driven to provide needs for our survival and success. While we may acknowledge a non-physical domain it often remains in the background as more immediate issues demand our attention.

Despite this vision of life, most people do believe in a connection to a higher, non-tangible consciousness. So how does this all connect and exist? Here's my take on it, whether correct or not, it is, nevertheless, a model I can comprehend and live with.

- First there was Universal Consciousness, it always was and always will be (God, Universal Whole).
- At some point God created Individualized Consciousness (Spirit).
- Spirit then begot Consciousness Personified (Man)
- Man created his material world (Ego)

The Urantia Book offers some further insight, "The second generation of the soul is the first of a succession of personality manifestations of spiritual and progressing existences, terminating only when this divine entity attains the source of its existence, the personal source of all existence, God, the Universal Father. "

I walked outside to a cloudless sky, with an embracing sun high above me. The smell of fresh cut grass still hung in the air, as birds were chirping their melodious songs, a perfect time to walk along Cherry Creek Trail to seek out a rock and meditate to its mini waterfall's peaceful burble. A slight breeze kissed my face as I sat and closed my eyes while Cherry Creek continued its tranquil song. I breathed deeply and was quickly transported to a world of beauty and peace. Subliminally, a voice beckons me onward.

"You are about to embark on a journey.
You are about to touch your inner soul.
You are about to feel the essence of God.
Relax, get comfortable.
Enjoy the experience of who you really are.
Deep within you lies the essence of God.
Relax, get comfortable.
Answers are waiting for you."

I am standing on a hill,
Overlooking a valley of sunflowers.
The flowers cover every square inch
And dance in beautiful unison.
"Welcome to the valley of peace and love."
The message resonates in my mind.
In the distance a figure appears,
Is it male or female?
It doesn't matter.
The figure walks slowly towards me,
As I descend from the hill to meet it.
I can feel the love.
I can feel the peace.
The flowers separate to open a path for me.
The figure's long, flowing robe
Gives it the appearance as if it were floating.
I can feel the emanation of warmth from the figure.
I can feel the emanation of love from the figure.
"I am Teacher."
As I come near, Teacher embraces me.
"Welcome to the Valley of Peace and Love,
What brings you here?"
"Who am I? Why am I here?"
"You are one with God," comes the reply.
"Nothing else matters, nothing can take it away from you.
Feast in God's goodness and not the chaos of the world.
Do not attempt to define God,
He can only be experienced."
I look into his eyes, they are radiating love;
I listen to his words; they are conveying eternal truths;
And I feel his touch; it is enveloping me in peace.
"Love is all that matters," he whispers,
"You don't have to search, it is already within you.
Open your heart, free your mind and follow the path within.

You are blessed, now and forever more.
It's that simple."
He kissed me on the forehead and turned to go.
"Thank you," I called as a tear traced down my cheek.
"For the love and insight you have given me."
I knew more answers would come later
But it was time to return to the top of the hill.
I stand there alone,
Overlooking the Valley of Sunflowers.

I could hear my voice calling me back.
I left the Valley of Sunflowers
And returned to the rock at Cherry Creek
Knowing the love of God will stay with me
And the love of God will nourish me.
I breathed deeply and opened my eyes slowly,
Remembering where I'd been,
Remembering who I truly am,
An expression of God.
In the distance I could hear
Teacher, "Never forget. Namaste"

As I slowly arose from my meditative perch, I noticed the grass was greener, the water more soothing and the birds more melodious. I could see and smell and hear nature's exquisiteness. Above all, I understood our purpose in this world was to experience life to its fullest. We are free to choose the fulfillment of life by either following the deep, dark tunnel of the ego or crossing the spiritual bridge to enlightenment. The good news is both paths lead back to the spiritual Oneness from whence we came; there can be no other way.

Chapter - 13

Love From Beyond

"Life, as we know it, is the emergence of spirit in form. Spirit manifest in the physical always returns to Spirit."

—Spirit

I walked into "All Things God" barely hearing the bell as I opened the door. Malachi was nowhere to be seen and I headed towards the back where Hannah kept her office.

It was small while offering a setting of comfort. Two chairs with soft, plush pillows framed a small, round table whose gold, silver and purple cloth reached the floor. In the middle stood a diffuser, misting essential oils into the air. Pictures of loving spirits, majestic animals and wild flowers adorned the walls, while low lights added a calming ambiance to the room. In the background a flutist was offering his rendition of "Amazing Grace."

"Hi, welcome," a soft, calming voice interrupted the flutist's recital.

"Hi, hi," I stumbled surprisingly as I turned around to meet Hannah.

There was no doubt she was a reincarnation of an ancient shaman whose knowledge of healing and spiritual things made them respected, and often feared, in their community. A hint of gray was beginning to appear in her dark, long-flowing hair that settled in the middle of her back. Without any makeup, she looked older than I believed she was but it didn't detract from her natural beauty. Her deep-seated eyes looked like they were able to pierce anyone's armor of self defense and extract one's deepest held secrets; and yet they were filled with kindness and compassion.

Probably a shade over five feet, she moved effortlessly and assuredly; she appeared to know what she wanted and wasn't afraid to get it. Her toe-length dress was an abstract of blues and greens with a touch of gold here and there. Resting on her shoulders was a white and gold wrap whose fringes, much like the tzitzit of prayer shawls, almost reached the floor while serving as a reminder to think of God at all times. I did sense a certain air of self-assuredness and confidence in her demeanor, probably nurtured by her superior mystic intellect and acumen. She could be your best friend or your worst enemy; the choice was up to you.

"Come in and make your self comfortable. I heard you met my daughter at Garden of the Gods a while back."

"Yes, she was meditating on a boulder facing Pikes Peak while I was doing some landscape photography."

"And you're here, as I understand, to see if we can contact your son who passed not too long ago."

"Yes," I replied.

"Have a seat and we'll get started."

I almost sank into one of the armchairs, while relishing its comfort. Hannah joined me in the other chair and began to close her eyes. "Give me your hands and we'll begin with a short prayer."

> "Dear God, we are gathered here to make contact
> With the dearly departed John.
> We know your house is filled with grace and well being
> And is a haven for eternal joy and peace.
> Let the spiritual John come through today
> To help ease our sorrow.
> And so it is."

Hannah turned out the lights until a single candle was left burning, as the lilac fragrance of the essential oil grew a bit stronger as "Amazing Grace" faded into the background. The candle began to flicker. For a moment my mind wandered back to an unforgettable time when I stood before a filled funeral home where every seat was taken. It was standing room only! Through the eerie silence, I could see people in the hallway straining to get a look inside. Low lights and an abundance of flowers added to the farewell messages on everyone's mind. And then there were the tears, silently tracing tracks on half the faces looking at me. Father Joseph had just completed his prayers of mourning and I felt it necessary to say a few words.

"That is not Johnny lying over there," I began while pointing at the coffin behind me, "he is not here, that is only his physical body you see. He is in a place where unimaginable joy abounds. Johnny is home, where he belongs. There is no suffering at God's side, only unbridled joy."

These words came remarkably easy for me despite my legs feeling like rubber and the threat of tears being dammed behind a stoic demeanor that refused to give in. Nobody moved or said a word. If it weren't for the occasional sniffle one would have thought this was all an illusion. It certainly felt that way to me. Reality, it seemed, had yet to set in.

"On behalf of our family and myself, I would like to thank you all for taking the time to say your farewells to my son. I'm sure he's smiling down at us in his mischievous way, grateful for your support and remembrance. But he also wants you to know the body you see here no longer belongs to him. He is now in his eternal resting place where peace and love abounds. Thank you again."

Silence continued for a few seconds after I sat down before people were comfortable enough to move around and whisper amongst themselves. And then the procession line began; one after the other, family, friends and strangers came to me to extend their condolences and sorrow for my loss. Some had tears flowing down their faces and others could barely speak, but their message of sorrow was etched in their faces. It was a message more powerful than words.

Internment took place the following day at one of the mausoleums at Pine Lawn Cemetery in Farmingdale. Looking at the coffin covered with flowers, I was still in a state of shock over the events of the last few days. My youngest son was being laid to rest and neither hope nor prayers would bring him back. Through clenched teeth, the dam I built behind my eyelids continued to hold firm. Holding my arm around Jannette to offer her comfort was more for the benefit of my rubbery legs threatening to give out at any moment. Looking back, it was my willingness to lean on an Almighty God whom I barely knew, which saw me through. But His support could not eradicate the feeling of loss that would follow me around from day to day. Finally, as my head rested upon my pillow that night, the dam gave way and the flood of tears began to flow.

Hannah interrupted my thoughts. She had a message for me from Johnny.

I listened intently as she began to speak, "I am in the most beautiful place imaginable. Your mountains cannot compare to the beauty existing here. More so, you don't just delight in their majestic beauty through your vision, one can feel their majesty. Here all five senses and then some, work in unison to give you a total, multi-dimensional experience. Here the encounters are total, never partial. You are immersed in the experience, whatever it is. And nothing, absolutely nothing, is ever less than supreme enjoyment. There are no problems, there are no issues, there is only good, only love, only truth.

"Yes I left unexpectedly, but I needed to. I was falling into a great abyss. I was following a road of self-destruction. Believe me when I say I would have become an addict and as such, my life would have been abysmal and it would have hurt the girls more than the way I decided to end it all. You, or anyone else, could not have helped me. I did not know how to fight the demons in my head. My only resource was to use drugs to quell the emotional and psychological pain. I am truly sorry for anyone's current pain, but I am in a much better place. I am home. And, as you know, I have always longed for a home where I could finally feel comfortable, feel loved and joy. This is where I am.

This is where we will all be eventually. Take care of the girls; I will be with you. If you need me or want something let me know; I will not let you down. Love from beyond."

Tears were welling in my eyes when Hannah handed me a piece of paper with a poem by Shannon Lee Moseley.

> Don't grieve for me, for now I'm free.
> I'm following the path God has chosen for me.
> I took His hand when I heard Him call;
> I turned my back and left it all.
> I could not stay another day,
> To laugh, to love to work or play.
> Tasks left undone must stay that way;
> I've found new peace at the end of the day.
> If my parting has left a void,
> Then fill it with remembered joys.
> A friendship shared, a laugh, a kiss;
> Oh yes, these things, I too will miss.
> Be not burdened with times of sorrow,
> Look for the sunshine of tomorrow.
> My life's been full, I savored much;
> Good friends, good times, a loved one's touch.
> Perhaps my time seems all too brief;
> Don't lengthen your time with undue grief.
> Lift up your heart and peace to thee.
> God wanted me now - He set me free.

As I arose to leave, Hannah saw the tears and came to embrace me. One embrace had never before been so meaningful. I felt her warmth, her love, her peace. It felt like I was enveloped in the Light of God whose peace surpasses all understanding; I instantly knew my home was not of this world. My tears dried up and my pain was replaced by an unbridled joy and knowing my time here was only temporary before we are all called home. I looked at Hannah, wiping tears from my eyes.

"It's OK to feel sad and miss him, but remember it's not OK to feel guilty. It was his choice to leave, for whatever reason. The important thing to understand is our time here is temporary and our purpose often misunderstood. We will all return to who we really are, spiritual beings basking in the loving Oneness. Johnny is there right now, just like he told you and, best of all, you can reach out to him at any time. Not only is he here for you, but also his daughters, his family and friends. Send him your love and he will surely send it back."

"Thank you," I replied, gathering my senses.

"Listen for his messages during the quiet times, he has much to offer you. Keep your heart and mind open. "

"Thank you, again," I replied, forcing a smile. Hanging my head, I left the shop as the flutist's melancholy "Amazing Grace" echoed in my mind.

Chapter - 14

The God Dichotomy

*"Know who you truly are and you will know
that all else is an illusion.
You can know a thing spiritually only by becoming it."*
—Neville

Classes were rapidly coming to an end, yet I had the distinct feeling the best was yet to come. Many topics had been discussed, yet how it all fit into a Universal Truth was missing. As I entered the classroom, Malachi had already written the topic of the day, "The God Dichotomy" on the whiteboard. Everyone was already seated as I gathered my writing pads and pens, ready to take notes.

"Today's class is about 'The God Dichotomy,' a very common misconception existing in every corner of this planet. Let me begin by stating, unequivocally, there is no such thing as a God dichotomy. It is something we humans have created long ago and still adhere to today. God is! God never was nor ever will be. God simply is. That, in itself, dispels any type of dichotomy, for to have a dichotomy there must be two states of opposites. Even within the singular state of "God is" exist only love and truth and joy. Again, no opposites exist, hence no dichotomy."

"If a God dichotomy doesn't exist, why are we talking about it?" Paul asked.

"Because we think it does," Malachi responded.

"How so?" Paul continued.

"When we first began this class," Malachi began, "we were under the impression God was an external being doing whatever gods do. Our job was to bring homage to this deity and in return we would receive the assurance, forgiveness, assistance or whatever is necessary to exist, survive and excel in our human environment. The God dichotomy exists solely in the human condition. It exists in the various belief systems and dogmas surrounding the existence of God. Where is God? Who is God? What is God? These are all valid questions we raise about a deity we prescribe to. Inherent in these questions, however, lies a belief of separation. As such, God has been deemed to exist in a place where heavenly bliss abounds rather than a place deep within the psyche. Therein lies the God dichotomy: we humans believe His existence ranges from without to within.

"As different as we are as a people of this planet, our beliefs are even more diverse, especially when it comes to the understanding, worshipping and believing in a supreme being. God is a deity whose supreme knowledge and power represents the penultimate ascension of man's consciousness and understanding. In most religious beliefs God is the pinnacle of all there is and is worshipped or lauded in a variety of ways. Not only is God understood differently in different religions, but He is often perceived differently within a singular mainstream religion. Christianity, whose Bible is the holy document delivering the Word of God, views its God differently than Judaism or Hinduism. Are we to assume the god of each religion is different, has different values, likes and dislikes? Of course not! There is only one God and it doesn't matter what you call Him."

"So how did the concept of God originate?" Mary asked.

"While I understand your question Mary, your foundation is incorrect. God didn't originate, He always was and always will be. But to answer your question, let me read you a poem called 'The Evolution of God':

There once was a god
Who was the sun
Causing all things to grow.
Statues were built
To earn his grace, and
Keeping rivers to flow.

There once was a god
Who controlled the sun
Keeping people at bay.
Sacrifices were made
To earn his love and
Keep the light of day.

There once was a god
Who came from the sun
To protect his people from harm.
Armies were built
Which he led
To protect their precious farms.

There once was a god
Who understood the sun
And taught his people to pray.
They lifted him up
To exalted state
And prayed to him every day.

There once was a god
Who glowed like the sun
Spreading a message of love.
Dogmas were spun
Like heaven and hell
So we might join him above.

> But there is a God Who is the sun
> And all that we can see. He sends us love
> And truth and grace
> And lives in you and me.

"So it appears gods were created to facilitate a need like sun for warmth, rain for plants, protection against invaders, and so on. Does anyone see the fallacy of all this?"

It was Sarah who stated the obvious, using her hands for added clarity, "In all cases, God resides outside of us. He is out there, not in here."

"Absolutely!" Malachi beamed. "That's the great God dichotomy and it was totally created by man eons ago and, unfortunately, is still the common belief today."

"Wait a minute," Paul interjected, "what about the forgiveness of sin through Jesus Christ which is the precursor to eternal life?"

"It's all well and good if you choose to believe it, but it's not necessary. As we discussed previously, if there is a sin it's our belief in separation from God. But God's love is unconditional so there's nothing to forgive. Forgiveness, like judgment, is a human action used to appease ourselves, not God," Malachi replied.

"You've just invalidated all the Christian Church stands for and all the good God does through His church," Paul retorted.

"Let me be clear," Malachi began, "the church, whatever denomination, was created by men to spread a message of salvation to people. While that is a good thing, it is not required, nor is it accurate. The dichotomy is God does not reside outside you, but rather inside you and me and every human being and every living thing."

"So God resides within every human being, including the worst criminals this world has ever produced?"

"That is true, Paul."

"So those criminals will also go to heaven whether they have asked for forgiveness or not?" Paul pressed on.

"While it may seem unfair, it is, nevertheless, true," Malachi assured.

"So if everyone is saved, regardless, why bother having a church?" Paul asked.

"The purpose of the church is to make us all aware of the goodness and love that resides within God and is available to anyone. All we have to do is search within ourselves to find our God center. God exists within us and we exist within the Oneness. We exist within Him, and He exists within us. There is no separation!"

Paul was already gathering his belongings before Malachi had finished speaking.

Getting up he affirmed a final, "I don't think so," and walked out of the room.

It took about a minute before Malachi recovered enough to continue. "God is a very simple and easily understood Being. However, lifelong teachings of dogmas and values are often difficult to overcome. I can assure you Paul will find his way, as we all will eventually."

"So the God dichotomy is nothing more than understanding He resides within each one of us and not outside of us?" Joanne asked.

"Exactly, it's that simple. The problem we have is accepting it. History has established the church and a dogma that has continued to identify us as subjects of God requiring His forgiveness before we can bask in His love. Let me be emphatic, His love is unconditional and has already been bestowed upon us. All we need to do is open ourselves to it. Look within, that's where you'll find it!

"Once we fully come to realize we are individualized expressions of the Universal Whole, most commonly called God, and He is infinite and His love is unconditional, then we can truly begin to understand the nature of God and our purpose in this mortal lifetime. Let me begin by saying although we're spiritual in nature, we are not here to grow spiritually. As temporal beings we cannot grow spiritually, we can only awaken to our spiritual nature.

"But what is infinite and unconditional love? Infinite implies a never ending state and as such, we must surmise God is continually growing through our experiences and, since He is synonymous with love, His love, not only never ends, but never stops growing as well. For if He should ever stop growing in any manner or form, He would no longer be infinite nor would His love be infinitely unconditional.

"So then, what and how does our relationship with the Divine exist? As an individualized expression of God, every act we partake in has a spiritual effect. Every step you make and every breath you take is a moment of now and, as such, is a moment where God's love grows. If you're happy and loving and peaceful, God is receptive to your feelings of love and His love grows accordingly. If you're in a space of lies and deceit, God's love will grow as He showers you with empathy, compassion and forgiveness. Yes, God's forgiveness is instantaneous; he doesn't sit back to ponder your situation or predicament before forgiving you. Understand, you never have to ask God for forgiveness it has already happened; instead, shower Him with gratitude and thanksgiving for these are acts of love. Unconditional Love never needs forgiveness.

"Every action you have taken is, therefore, a success story simply because every one of your actions has grown God's love. Through you, God continues to grow His infinite nature. It is true of every temporal entity in this universe. Because His love is unconditional, we can go through life knowing all is well, regardless of our biased past, regardless of our selfish nature and regardless of our judgments. Our lives can never be considered a failure because at every moment we are connected to the Divine who will never abandon us. The dichotomy of God only exists because of our inability to comprehend that our temporal existence is a spiritual manifestation in form. Therefore, success, being preordained, is never about our worldly accomplishments but about our ability to express God and grow His love."

Malachi handed out a sheet of paper and asked one of us to read it aloud. It was several quotes from Neal Donald Walsh's book *Conversations With God, Book 3*. Mary raised her hand and began to read:

"It's important to learn about Divine Dichotomy and understand it thoroughly if you are to live in our universe with grace. Divine Dichotomy holds that it is possible for two apparently contradictory truths to exist simultaneously in the same space. Now on your planet people find this difficult to accept. They like to have order, and anything that does not fit into their picture is automatically rejected. For this reason, when two realities begin to assert themselves and they seem to contradict one another, the immediate assumption is that one of them must be wrong, false, untrue. It takes a great deal of maturity to see, and accept, that, in fact, they might both be true. Yet in the realm of the absolute—as opposed to the realm of the relative, in which you live—it is very clear that the one truth which is All There Is sometimes produces an effect which, viewed in relative terms, looks like a contradiction."

"Thank you, Mary. Joanne, can you read the next one please?"
"Yes," and she began to read:

God: "The greatest Divine Dichotomy is the one we are looking at now. There is only One Being, and hence, only One Soul. And, there are many souls in the One Being. Here's how the dichotomy works: You've just had it explained to you that there is no separation between souls. The soul is the energy of life that exists within and around (as the aura of) all physical objects. In a sense, it is that which is "holding" all physical objects in place. The "Soul of God" holds in the universe, the "soul of man" holds in each individual human body."
Neale Donald Walsch: "The body is not a container, a "housing," for the soul; the soul is a container for the body."
God: "That's right."
Neale Donald Walsch: "Yet there is no "dividing line" between souls— there is no place where "one soul" ends

and "another" begins. And so, it is really one soul holding all bodies."

God: "Correct."

Neale Donald Walsch: "Yet the one soul "feels like" a bunch of individual souls."

"And Sarah, would you be so kind to read the final excerpt of Neal Donald Walsh's book?"

"Certainly," as Sarah began to read:

"In ultimate reality there is no such thing as good and evil. In the realm of the absolute, there is only love. Yet in the realm of the relative you have created the experience of what you "call" evil, and you have done it for a very sound reason. You wanted to experience love, not just "know" that love is All There Is, and you cannot experience something when there is nothing else but that. And so, you created in your reality (and continue to do so every day) a polarity of good and evil, thus using one so that you might experience the other.

And here we have a Divine Dichotomy—two seemingly contradictory truths existing simultaneously in the same place. Specifically:

There is such a thing as good and evil. There is only Love."

"Thank you, Sarah. This has been a trying day for us all. Please understand I'm not attempting to convert anyone but just attempting to awaken the spirit residing within each one of us. I leave you with this verse from Luke 11:9-10: 'And so I tell you, keep on asking, and you will receive what you ask for. Keep on seeking, and you will find. Keep on knocking, and the door will be opened to you. For everyone who asks, receives. Everyone who seeks, finds. And to everyone who knocks, the door will be opened.'"

Chapter - 15

Teacher

"It does not matter how you meditate, it only matters that you meditate. Meditation is opening the channel of communication with your inner self and that is the passageway to God. Look within!"
—Spirit

I lay comfortably on my bed in a full supine position breathing deeply through my nose and exhaling fully through my mouth. It didn't take long before I found myself in my favorite mountaintop place overlooking a deep valley with a single tree, whose visible roots and bright green leaves adorning its symmetrical branches, served as my meditative transport system.

As usual, I was dressed in Native American buckskin with a single freedom feather in my headdress. This day I felt an urge to follow the tree downward towards its roots to explore the realm of objectivity. As always, my Spirit Guide came along to answer any questions and to provide me with protection.

On this journey we transported back in time. I saw a variety of historical scenes, stopping at the Jurassic Age for a closer look at the dinosaurs who dominated the landscape. Their enormous size was quite intimidating and I pleaded, "Let's move on from here."

It didn't take long before I found myself looking at the blue orb we call earth. Slowly at first and then more rapidly, the orb turned into a dot as the entire solar system and then the Milky Way disappeared before my eyes. What was left were the distant galaxies visible only through the most powerful telescopes. They also became smaller and smaller until, with one final "poof" there was nothing but a vast blackness.

"The big bang?" I asked.

"As best as you can understand," came to the reply. Within an instant, I found myself at my mountaintop place of comfort attempting to relive what I had just experienced. "Tomorrow we will climb the tree and experience the realm of subjectivity."

With my meditative travel still fresh in my mind, I quickly found my journal and began to write. Watching the earth disappear into the depths of the universe helped me realize the vastness of it all. And God is everywhere. Omnipresence had taken on a whole new meaning. This was only the objective world! Tomorrow I would visit the subjective realm.

The following evening I found myself at my mountaintop feeling a freedom seldom experienced in the material world. I climbed the tree to find myself in a place of white with only a marble bench before me. It was a place of intrinsic beauty difficult to fathom in a place dominated by one color. But it was more than just visual; it imbued a feeling of love and peace.

"Hello Hans, I'm Teacher," came a telepathic message as a being, also dressed in an all white robe appeared next to me, "we met at the Valley of Sunflowers."

"Hello, I remember," I replied without moving my lips, "why did you ask me to come here?"

"To help you understand that your objective world is not your true reality. You are spiritual in nature and your true home is this realm of the subjective."

"You mean this is my real home?" I asked.

"It is everyone's and everything's home. Every objective being or thing originates in the subjective. All that is flows through Divine Energy."

"So there is no death or hell?" I asked.

Teacher smiled and he seemed to even chuckled a bit, "What you call death is simply a transition from the material realm to the spiritual. It's you returning home. Hell, as you know it, is a state of mind. It is your perception of being separate from God." He let me absorb this information before continuing, "Whenever you have any questions or need to replenish your energy levels, you can meet me here. But you don't have to be here to contact me. Just close your eyes and ask your question. I will always answer."

I contemplated his words for a while and then asked, "How do I replenish my energy?"

"You see the building over there?" Just then, what seemed like a white church with a steeple disappearing into the clouds emerged.

Without saying a word I headed toward the church and the doors opened for me to enter. I found myself in a large circular room with a myriad of round symbols hanging on the walls. Some looked familiar like the Christian cross and the yin-yang, while others appeared foreign to me. As best as I could fathom, they were religious symbols of varying kinds representing beliefs throughout the world, or possibly the universe.

My eyes turned upwards gazing into the never-ending steeple above me. I centered myself beneath it, closed my eyes, spread my arms and opened my heart. A jolt of pure energy instantly engulfed me, refreshing my soul and energizing my heart. It was pure bliss. After my soul had been rejuvenated, I could feel rays of light leaving my essence and connecting with all of the round symbols adorning the walls. This energy, I found, did not just belong to me but to all beings. The energy I was feeding into the symbols soon came back to me in what became a continuous cycle of love and peace. The more I gave, the more I received. I learned that by giving, I will receive more than I could ever imagine. I finally understood the Oneness joining us together in one giant embrace of Love and Light.

I teleported back out to the marble bench where Teacher was waiting for me. I didn't have to explain what had happened, he already knew. "Here your energy levels will never diminish for love is the most powerful force. Only in your material world where problems and issues continually attack the psyche will people lose their spiritual insight. You can always go within to re-energize or, if you wish, you can always visit our temple. Close your eyes and open your mind and embrace the figure of truth and goodness appearing before you."

I did as Teacher asked and the face of Jesus, in all its glory, appeared before me. I felt calm and at ease with love flowing throughout my being. After a while his face began to change. The beard remained but the face was no longer Jesus. It was Osama bin Laden. He was also smiling at me while continuing to fill my essence with peace and love. After a few moments I returned to my place on the marble bench fully energized. "Why did Jesus turn to bin Laden?" I asked.

"To let you know that all people have their roots in the God center. All people are spiritually pure regardless of how they appear or behave in your material world," Teacher replied.

"If all of us have our roots within the Love of God, why can some be so deceitful and evil?" I asked.

"You are all given freedom of choice and your mind is an empty shell when you first make your appearance in your world. You are taught by other humans how to survive and co-mingle in a competitive world. In your world, to experience goodness one must understand evil, its opposite. To understand compassion one must comprehend pain and suffering. Because all people are given free will, everyone reacts differently to events and happenings around them. This doesn't mean people are good or bad, it just means some react differently to circumstances based on their presumptive needs. What never changes is everyone's connection to Universal Love. Whether you are the next Jesus, Osama bin Laden, Buddha, Hitler or a beggar in the street, your home is the Oneness and your essence is Divine Love."

"But death and suffering are such drastic measures, they shouldn't be bestowed on any person." I interjected.

"What you define as suffering is nothing more than your perception of separation from God. What you define as death is quite simply a doorway returning you to the Oneness, where you belong. Judging life in the material world through human filters ignores who you really are. Once mankind comes to understand this simple truth, all evil will evaporate and goodness, peace and harmony will envelop human existence. For there can be no other outcome as God is unconditional Love."

"So it's never God who has to change or act to straighten out our chaotic world. It's up to us to awaken to our spiritual nature and return to who we really are. And if we are in a position of suffering and need, we are, in reality, offering a pathway for others to realize there is a better way, thereby helping them to search for who they really are," I interjected.

"Pretty close," Teacher replied, "God has also given you the power to create and how you use this power will determine how you establish your environment. But remember, regardless how difficult or hopeless your journey appears to be, never and I mean never will you ever be abandoned by the Divine Goodness. Your were born of Love and you shall return to Love."

I embraced Teacher and saw a familiar twinkle in his eye as we parted, "Thank you, Teacher."

"One more thing before we part," Teacher began, "your Todd Michael who wrote *The Evolution Angel* has a very simple technique to reach within when your free time is limited. A silent, respectful chant of, 'Yahweh' will help you journey to your God center. When you focus on your heart while chanting, the experience will magnify itself. 'Yahweh' will help to balance your life and help you achieve harmony."

"Thank you, again, Teacher."

As I returned to my mountaintop I could see the auras surrounding the plants and trees and birds. All were enveloped in a loving energy knowing no bounds. God was everywhere and everything contributed to the loving scene before me. Nothing was more important; nothing was greater. There was only the Oneness grown out of Love.

Chapter - 16

I AM

*"There is no science that can identify God;
there is no philosophy that can define God.
God cannot be explained; God can only be experienced."*
—Spirit

"I am consciousness can only speak in the present tense."
—Neville

As I walked in early for our final class, hoping to privately speak with Malachi about my meditation and meeting with Teacher, Paul had, however, beaten me to the punch. He was speaking quietly with Malachi and I could tell they were smoothing things over after the eruption from the last class. "I'm glad to see you back, Paul," was all I could hear Malachi say. Paul smiled and nodded before taking his seat.

It seemed everyone was glad to see Paul return as it lifted the air of divisiveness that had settled over the class since he stormed out of the room the previous week. Before the lecture began, Paul asked to address the rest of us to further clear the air, "I must apologize for my outburst and angry exit during the last class. As I'm sure you are aware I'm a deep believer of the Christian religion and as such I quite often approach any religious dialogue with a stubborn sense of bias. I've done quite a bit of soul searching this past week and have come to realize Jesus' teachings were all inclusive and not exclusive. Therefore, I do believe some of his messages may have become skewed over the years. While I will maintain my Christian faith, I will, however, continue to keep an open mind to the discussions we will have here. Again, my apologies."

"Good to see you back, Paul," Joanne offered, "it's not the same without you."

"Regardless of your belief, I'm glad to see you back. It's our diverse convictions, which help to make this class special. Welcome back," Sarah chimed in.

"Good to see you," I offered.

Mary simply added, "Ditto to all of what was said."

Malachi turned to the class and began to speak, "At the beginning of this class, I asked you all to finish the 'I Am' quote. Let me go around the room again and ask you all to tell me who you are, and please qualify your statement. Paul, why don't you start us off?"

"I Am Paul, a son of God. God is the Father and I am a son of God, in fact we are all sons of God. He created us and we, as a result, are His children."

"Very good, Sarah, how about you?"

"I Am Sarah, a personification of God. God is a spiritual being as are we. We are spiritual beings having a human experience. Within us, exists a tiny and divine mustard seed connecting us all to our source, God."

"Very nice, Sarah. And what do you have to say, Mary?"

"I Am Mary, an expression of God. Since God is a spiritual being, the only way He can experience the physical world is through His creations like me. We do have free will and are so caught up with the expectations and requirements of this society we often lose sight of our connection to Him."

"And that is truly unfortunate. Thank you, Mary. Joanne, what do you have to say?"

"I Am Joanne, the consciousness of God. God is pure consciousness and it is through consciousness that we are connected to God. This consciousness gives us the ability to think, reason and understand our environment. But we often lose sight of our origin and try to deal with day-to-day issues, thereby forgetting who we really are."

"Excellent! Hans, what do you have to say?"

"I Am God!"

Malachi hesitated a bit, probably expecting a bit more. "And how have you come to that conclusion?"

I imagined all eyes staring at me as the collar on my collarless shirt began tightening around my neck. Why did I have to be so brazen? "Well," I began, choosing my words carefully while avoiding Paul's piercing eyes, "it's simple logic as I can see. God is consciousness and we have consciousness. God is also eternal and omnipresent. Omnipresence means He is in every person, animal, plant and inanimate object. Every atom has God consciousness. It has to be! Otherwise He would not be omnipresent. Keeping this in mind, we are all imbued in the Oneness that is God and we all exist within the God consciousness. We are not separated from God and, therefore, we exist in the same Oneness, hence, we are all God."

"Interesting," Malachi began, "sounds heretical. You wouldn't have survived very long in old Jerusalem, Caiaphas would have seen to that."

Malachi turned to the white board and began by drawing a circle. "This is the Universal Whole." Within the circle he drew a heart with the tip of it meeting the center of an infinity sign. "This is my symbol for God, Infinite Love. That is what the Oneness is, never ending love." He continued drawing stick figures holding hands, attached to the outer surface of the circle. It was the exact same symbol I first saw on the window of his shop in Evergreen. "These stick figures represent us, humans. We feel disconnected, separated from Source, when, in reality, we are all connected to the Oneness. And because we are all connected to God, we are all united in one big brotherhood, whether we like it or not."

He turned to look at us, pausing, I'm sure, for effect before continuing, "You are all right! Let us never forget we are all united in the Oneness; we all have our origin in Divine Love; we all share the Eternal Consciousness; we are all the I Am."

I began to realize Malachi's spoken word had already formulated itself in my mind. What I thought he spoke; my thoughts mirrored his lesson. We were mentally and spiritually connected. He realized it as well as he looked at me, smiled and winked. It was I who was giving the lesson through Malachi; our minds seemed to have fused into one. Starke's *The Third Appearance* was playing out in our classroom.

His words were spoken with a clarity I had never known as my inner and outer selves were no longer separate entities; I had been born again. I closed my eyes and internally visualized the words and ideas Malachi was speaking. For once they made perfect sense. There were no questions or moments of doubt, only a sense of belonging and understanding the Truth. My transformation was complete! The caterpillar in my cocoon was emerging like a beautiful butterfly longing to spread its wings and fly in total freedom while enjoying the world around it. I was free at last, no longer bound by earthly bonds of rules and expectancies.

As I kept my eyes closed I could feel myself drift into a deep meditative state. Finally, I had entered the world of grace where only love, and peace existed. While my initial journey into the world of grace was filled with love and warmth, this time my state of grace was enhanced with a knowing and understanding of what the Universal Oneness was all about. Omniscience, omnipotence and omnipresence were no longer concepts, I understood their reality; no, I was being in their reality!

Malachi was still talking to the class and I was watching him through closed eyes. My soul was listening while teleporting its message of universal oneness and brotherhood. Then, without hesitation, I could feel my soul join with his; we had become one! My objective universe had morphed to my subjective roots. My tangible reality had given way to who I really am, a spiritual being enveloped in a bliss of Oneness unbeknown in a world of physical deception. Finally, I understood Love is the only true reality.

As I gradually came out of my transient state, I could see Malachi look at me and smile. He nodded his head slightly in a knowing fashion. His final words to the class were, "We are all connected in the Oneness called God!"

A silence had befallen all of the students who were seemingly trying to fathom what had just occurred. Had each one of us had the same experience? Had each one of us connected with our inner selves, magically transporting each one to personally experience the Oneness in his/her own distinctive way? Was Malachi more than a gateway to my soul, but a manifestation of my own inner self? Malachi, I am sure, was a messenger from God delivering, to each one of us, exactly what we needed to hear and to remove whatever barriers we had constructed so we could emerge as our true spiritual selves.

Malachi hesitated a bit, looking each one of us directly in the eye before continuing, "I would like to thank each one of you for taking this class. Whatever you do, don't just believe who you really are. Know it! Believing has its roots in separation while knowing embraces the Oneness. I hope to see you all again soon. Namaste!"

We all left without speaking or saying good byes, there was no need; we all understood. Today, my life was forever changed by a man whose message was filled with Truth, delivered with Love and immersed in spiritual Joy. Today I understood beyond any reasonable doubt this sacred truth: "God is, therefore I Am!"

Chapter - 17

The Revelation

"Did you ever sincerely endeavor to talk with the spirit of your own soul? ...Every honest attempt of the material mind to communicate with its indwelling spirit meets with certain success."
—The Urantia Book

Another mile before the Evergreen Parkway exit, traffic had made my journey along Interstate 70 longer than usual and kept my stomach churning. I felt it important to get some finality to my beliefs, judgments and insights lingering in the back of my mind. Malachi's final class left me with more questions than I had anticipated. What was the melding of our minds all about? Who was this man?

A half hour later I found myself entering the shop to the tune of its singular bell. "Hi, Hans, what brings you here?" It was Hannah standing behind the counter looking up from some paperwork.

"Hi, Hannah. I'm looking for Malachi. Is he here?"

She stopped searching through her papers and with a furrowed brow asked, "Who?"

"Malachi," I replied.

"Who's Malachi?" she asked.

"Malachi, he owns this store. I met him here a couple of months ago."

"I'm sorry, Hans, but there is no Malachi here. Never has been. Are you sure you're at the right place?" Hannah, suddenly standing up straight and tilting her head, questioned.

"How could that be?" I asked, not sure whether my mind was playing tricks on me. "He was here. I spoke to him and took his class at the Academy for Lifelong Living."

"I don't know about the class, but there has never been a Malachi who owned or worked in this store."

"This is impossible," I muttered to myself. "Are you sure?" Looking in the corner I could see Malachi's totem pole like walking stick. "The cane, that's Malachi's cane!" I blurted.

Looking around and spotting the walking stick, Hannah responded solemnly, "It used to belong to my father who passed away about a year ago."

"But that can't be!"

Hannah could sense my agitation and sudden nervousness. "Here, sit down. Talk to me."

I explained how I had come to take Malachi's class and how I met him here during one of my photography trips to Lake Evergreen; how he had come to enlighten me about my spiritual misgivings and renewed my faith in the Oneness. Finally I told her how he and I apparently merged our souls during his final class.

"This is all very interesting," she began, "I must assume you had another spiritual experience similar to the one you had when you journeyed to the Light. These experiences are very vivid and leave a total sense of realism in individuals."

"Are you saying I dreamed about all of this?"

"Not dreamed necessarily, but experienced on a subconscious level. Your subconscious mind is filled with memories, beliefs and fears all making an imprint on your reality. It can, without your awareness directly affect what happens in your life. Dr. Joseph Murphy, who wrote *The Power Of Your Subconscious Mind* stated quite simply, "The subconscious mind is ruled by suggestion, it accepts all suggestions — it does not argue with you — it fulfills all suggestions.' If your internal self had been in turmoil over the loss of your son and its resulting questioning of God and the spiritual realm, I could understand how this may have triggered your subconscious to respond."

"So, none of this is true?"

"No, I didn't say that," Hannah replied. "Just because there is no tangible proof of your experience doesn't mean it's not true. Your journey to the Light was not tangible, but yet you know it happened and you're not questioning its validity. Look at Malachi in the same sense. He exists, but not in this material world. He may very well be a guardian angel or spiritual guide who felt the need to get this message to you. It could have been a dream or during meditation, but regardless how it came to pass, the important thing is the message was delivered."

"Was it possibly your father who came to me?" I asked unsurely.

"I don't think so. He was not a spiritual man. But then, all things are possible with God."

"So what do I do now?" I asked, totally perplexed.

"Go and meditate. Ask the question and, I'm sure, the answer will come to you."

I rose slowly, unsure whether to ask any more questions. Was I crazy? I mumbled a barely audible good-bye and left the store.

Arriving home I found a note from Jannette indicating she had tried to call me and was going out to eat with her friends. Hoping to speak with her about my shocking discovery I received an internal message to meditate. I headed up to the bedroom and resting my head on a pillow, I closed my eyes.

It didn't take long before I found myself at my familiar mountaintop surroundings. Breathing deeply, I felt myself in a totally relaxed condition looking forward to obtaining some answers. Climbing the tree to the higher spiritual level, I sat on the marble bench and waited for Teacher to appear.

It didn't take long and, as always, Teacher seemed to appear out of thin air. As usual, he was smiling broadly with glowing eyes that were both piercing and kind. His long, white robe moved majestically in a very slight breeze. "Hi, Hans," he began, "I assume you have some questions."

"Yes," I interrupted, "I found out Malachi doesn't exist, so who was he? Were all my interactions with him real?"

"Let me assure you all your interactions with Malachi were real, just like this meeting with me is. There are many levels of existence in the Realm of the Divine; your material world is only one of them. In fact it's the least spiritual of all. You might have heard of the seven planes of existence defining different dimensions of this universe and beyond. Vianna Stibal, one of your planet's famous spiritual teachers and healers who established the Theta Healing philosophy, identifies these levels: first are the inorganic minerals, crystals and rocks; the second plane exists of the organics, vitamins, plants and trees; the third plane consists of protein-based life forms including humans and other animals; the fourth plane is the realm of spirit, where spirits exist after death; the next plane is the dimension of divine beings such as Jesus and Buddha; the sixth plane is where the Laws that govern the universal fabric reside; and the final plane is where the Creator of All That Is exists, whose energy flows through all things. All these planes are interconnected and, of course, are filled with Divine Energy."

"Are you saying I had an experience in a dimension other than my physical one?"

"As best as you can understand. You asked the question of who you were during one of your meditations. Instead of just telling you, we sent you on a journey to answer your question. This journey enabled you to feel, see and hear who you really are. It's an experience you will remember much more readily than verbal responses. Your journey towards the Light was a similar experience. In *The Evolution Angel*, Todd Michael reminds us, 'When you are dealing with a messenger, you are dealing with God...Messengers are Spirit's way of revealing itself, of channeling itself in a way that can be safely tolerated by human beings.' Think about this for a moment. These messengers come in many forms and catch your attention in many ways. Messengers can take the form of humans, animals and even inanimate objects. The important thing to realize is the message is the primary intent, not the means."

"So, Malachi doesn't exist?"

Teacher laughed heartedly, "We are all expressions of the Divine. You are not Hans, just like I am not Teacher. We are simply spiritual energy having different types of experiences." After speaking, Teacher arose and stood in front of me with arms spread wide from his body. He began to glow as his vibration increased, becoming brighter and brighter. I could feel his love and joy radiate from within him; and then Teacher was unrecognizable as only a figure of light stood before me. Then the vibration slowed and the light began to fade until I recognized the figure before me.

My mouth was agape and my eyes wide open as I saw a young version of Malachi stand before me. "You're Malachi!"

"I am who you desire me to be."

Before I could ask one of the many questions formulating within me, Malachi's vibration increased again until a figure of light stood before me with a more intense feeling of love and joy. Again the vibration slowed until I recognized that impish grin. I jumped to my feet. "Johnny, you're Johnny!" I screamed as tears poured from my eyes and my younger son stood before me.

"I am whoever you need me to be."

I jumped to embrace my son. Overcome with joy and love, tears of joy erupted from within. I felt his love! I felt his joy! I could not only feel our embrace, I could see it! I could taste it! I could smell it! All my senses became acutely aware of the loving spirit I was embracing. Letting go of all inhibitions, I became completely vulnerable, yet I felt totally safe.

And then my son's vibration began to increase, reaching a point where I felt my heart would burst. I became aware of the Oneness and what it actually meant. With the increasing vibration I began to meld with the Divine Mind. I became aware of everything around me, from the smallest atom to the largest galaxy. Nothing was too large or too small. Nothing was inconsequential.

Everything was alive, basking in Love. I recognized the realm of the physical, the realm of the spiritual and the realm of the Divine. Everything mattered, every pebble, every insect and every blade of grass. Our physical world is, I learned, one giant organism ebbing and flowing in response to the highs and lows of individual expressions. I understood the need for the bin Ladens and Hitlers to help the planet grow in spiritual consciousness. It was through battles and famine that the earthly consciousness would raise to the level of enlightenment. And this was happening on all planets across the universe, across all universes.

I felt an all inclusive, infinite field of loving energy attempting to embrace all the physical species across the universes with the Oneness of Love. Time and time again, however, the embrace would be rejected as the physical realm would move deeper in its belief of separation. But the call to Love never stopped, until, inevitably, everyone would awaken to Spirit.

I came to realize that Johnny was not only my son, but he was my teacher as well. Malachi was also my teacher and my son. Everyone is my teacher as everyone is my son. These things can only be known in the Oneness.

My focus came back to the embrace as I felt the vibrations slowing. Tears did not stop as I came to the realization and burst out in a barely audible voice, "You're God!"

Malachi's vision re-entered my consciousness, "All beings are facets of the great Being of Beings which continually transforms and recycles itself. God is love, pure love." I felt the energy subside, regardless how hard I attempted to hold on. "Don't go, don't let this end," I implored telepathically.

"There is no need for fear, never forget, we are all one with God!" came the reassuring reply. "Welcome back to the Oneness."

Epilogue

I continued to embrace Divine Love as my essence received and returned the euphoric feeling of Oneness. There was no limit to the Love received or given. There was no limit to the joy and peace permeating throughout my body. But it wasn't my body anymore, it was my essence; I was connected to everyone and everything. Nothing was foreign to me; everything was as it should be. I saw with a clarity I had never known before. I felt with a sensuousness I had never experienced before. I breathed with a joyfulness I never knew existed. I communicated with a simplicity and transparency unknown in the realm of form. It all seemed so easy, surpassing all understanding. Everything was as it should be, nothing was out of place; everything was perfect.

In the distance I saw several forms approaching, their auras of love extending before them. Their warmth and love enveloped me well before they arrived. I recognized them immediately, not by their form or appearance but by my conscious connection to them. Approaching were my mother and father and son and my aunts and uncles who had long ago left the earthly plane of existence. They were welcoming me home, welcoming my return to who I really was, the I AM. When we embraced, the light surrounding us grew a hundred fold as love was given and received unconditionally. Here there was no judgment or need for forgiveness for Love only knows Love. Here the ego no longer existed for this was the realm of Divine Perfection.

Here there is a deeper understanding of who I really Am. I was no longer this individual form called Hans Benes; I was connected to the entire spirit world through the emblazoning power of Love. We all share in this Love and, as a result, we all grow in this Love. I gained a clear perspective of the interrelationship of all things. Nothing is inconsequential, nothing is a lesser than the whole. I began to understand that the root of all existence is Love. Omnipresence, omniscience and omnipotence were no longer difficult to understand concepts; they became simple realities imprinted in everyone's consciousness.

Freedom here was total and complete as each experience increased the universal conscious level of awareness. One could travel to the edge of the universe in an instant by just deeming it so. One could experience the forces of physics and their effects on things by just initiating a thought. One could comingle with other Spirits by just inviting them in. Nothing was impossible as all possibilities were just a conscious inspiration away.

There was a life review. It was not filled with judgment or reprimands; instead it was filled with loving understanding and purpose. I realized the vast majority of my lifetime was spent in separation, isolated from the loving spirit I really was. I understood my purpose in life was to awaken to my spiritual roots and return to the Oneness. I understood everyone was on a similar journey and the bond that held us together in the spiritual world was glaringly missing in the physical realm. I understood my fear of survival usurped my alacrity for brotherhood and love.

In the distance I saw flickering lights going on and off. "What are they?" I asked no one in particular.

"Souls returning to form," came the telepathic reply. "You may choose where or when you wish to visit the material world. It is entirely up to you."

For now, I decided, I will remain in my spiritual home and embrace the Love that is God. I will further enhance my empathic abilities as I get to welcome my spiritual brothers. Attaining knowledge is a never-ending process that serves to grow Love. Understanding and welcoming this growth, I look forward to a more successful visit to the realm of form. Until then, Namaste.

Afterword

"The mind of man is human, mortal,
but the spirit of man is divine, immortal."
—*The Urantia Book*

Let me reiterate my previous disclaimer, "There is no such thing as a God dichotomy!" God is all there is, He can never be anything different. Despite all our attempts to humanize the Divine, it will never happen. God is, it's as simplistic as it can get. This God dichotomy exists purely in the minds of man; it stems from our misunderstanding of who we really are. As we attempt to understand God, we tend to humanize He who cannot be humanized. We give superpowers to one who doesn't need them. We gladly send our shortcomings skyward pleading for forgiveness to One who cares not about our human faults, One who only knows us as loving spirits.

The God dichotomy exists within the framework of being human. We have created it to somehow appease our need for success or retribution. Once we have been forgiven for whatever transgression, we are free to transgress again with minimal guilt. It's a cycle, which works well for us: sin and forgiveness have become an integral piece of our lives. Searching for God out-there has blinded us to finding God with-in. Therein exists the great God dichotomy.

Life is beautiful! There is beauty in everything for those willing to behold it. The beggar on the street is a beautiful, spiritual being who has lost his way in a material world. The stark, nakedness of an uncaring city is a wonderful achievement of architectural creativity.

The secret to life is the way we approach it. Once we realize everyone and everything has a spiritual origin then we begin to look at things differently. We begin to realize the wonderment of creation, not only of the Divine's, but our own as well. Real beauty resides in everything, but those who only look with their eyes rarely see it. Open your heart and you will see beauty wherever you go.

You are a beautiful being for you are a creation of Divine inspiration. You are an expression of a Higher Power and, as a result, whatever you create has its roots within Spirit. Seize the moment! Recognize what's happening around you. Understand each event is an opportunity for growth. And as you grow, know you are guided by a higher power that will not let you fail. Know you are a co-creator of your life. Experience all life has to offer and your journey will be filled with joy and success. For what is the real purpose of our lives, other than to be filled with an unbridled happiness of achievement and self-esteem? Therein lies your fortune!

I have gone through much of my life focused on survival. Long ago my parents instilled Calvinistic ideals into my view of the world. "Work hard and good things will come to you," was one of their favorite mantras. It is a code by which they lived. And so I began to work hard, suppressing the thirst for lasting relationships and lightheartedness. But I worked, and I did it well.

As I grew older I began to realize there was more to life than working hard and earning money. I began to understand successful relationships were built on trust and love, not material wealth. I realized seeing my kids grow up was more important than working overtime. Unfortunately, this realization came too late to save my first marriage. Materialism will never trump a relationship based on common ideals, sharing, mutual respect and love.

It was during my second marriage I was introduced to spirituality. For too long I was under the impression dogmas and spirituality were one and the same. Nothing could have been further from the truth. I have come to realize God is not a being without, but rather a presence within. Life, as we know it, is the emergence of Spirit in form.

My existence, I have come to understand, is a sojourn in a physical world intent on creating a reality from which there is no escape. Our ego driven belief system continues to prioritize day to day living in a competitive and results driven environment. Who has the time for spirituality when the immediate needs demand to be satisfied? I grew up in a household of need where food, clothing and security dominated the survival system. God and Spirit were ideals dismissed long ago, while hard work was prioritized as a precursor to success.

As I grew, I began to absorb the same ideals my parents taught me. I began to look at my life and saw only tangible needs and success. Raising children and maintaining a respectable living environment was enabled by a well-entrenched financial system that measured accomplishments or failures. God was an afterthought.

All my life I have been searching for God in all the wrong places. My focus was deeply immersed in a material world, which continually moved the finish line as one need replaced another. Alas, my focus was always on outward issues and accomplishments. The peace of mind I had been seeking was always an issue away, as my self-worth was always driven by material things.

Along the way, I began to question things that were taken for granted. Critical thinking, I found, is a God given gift we all have received, yet rarely utilize. Asking why, how, when or where opens doors to new insights never imagined. This book is an exercise in critical thinking; the theories and beliefs proposed herein are the direct results of my questions to the Divine. Whether right or not, they are, nevertheless, concepts I feel comfortable with and they help formulate my spiritual beliefs. This book was not written to convert anyone to any ideology, but to open your mind to new possibilities. My hope is that everyone forms their own opinions and not baselessly accept or advance another's.

As a result of my questioning, there have been times when I've had great insights, times when messages came to me out of the blue, messages that were "dead on." There was also an experience. One I can only describe as a near death experience, only I wasn't dead, I was sleeping. It was so powerful that its incredible feeling of euphoria took days to subside. This occurrence, however, imbued an understanding our human existence is not the ultimate experience; there is an existence far surpassing our limited understanding of this tangible world. It has shown me there is a higher purpose to all life and we can tap into its energy here and now. This energy is filled with love and knowing and compassion and peace. It is the God energy within us all, which not only connects us to the Divine, but to every living being on this planet. And so I continue to search for this God-connection, within, which will break the chains of human expectancies and competitive superiority.

My life in this dimension will be short-lived compared to the immortal plane of Divine Presence. To understand we are spiritual by nature is key to understanding who we really are and our connection to the Universal Source is all that matters. God's omnipresence, omnipotence and omniscience reside within us all; all one needs to do is to internally tap into it. It is, unfortunately, a daunting task made more difficult by our demanding, judgmental society immersed in a materialistic existence, which seems to have little room for intangible principles. Remember, God is not an external deity demanding praise and adulation; He is an internal knowing residing within us all, who will gladly give us everything we desire. All we need to do is ask.

So, how exactly, do we speak with God? How can we ensure our message is received and heard? Simply stated, there is no correct way; there is no formality required or any rote response to memorize. God is always listening to you; there is never a moment He is too busy to take care of His flock. He knows who we really are; we, by and large, are blinded by a material existence requiring expected interactions to survive and succeed. The issue lies with us! It is never a God issue!

So, where do we begin? Talk to Him, recognize Him, embrace Him, and love Him. Say, "Hey God, how's it going?" If this is your comfort level, so be it. Get down on your knees and pray diligently and meditate responsibly. If this is your comfort level, so be it. Whatever you do, however you do it, reach out to Him. There is no right or wrong way to speak to God; it's a matter of mindset and self-introspection. God is with-in, He is never with-out.

Todd Michael, in his book *The Evolution Angel*, simply states, "When you pray, enter your closet, and when you have shut the door, pray to your Father which is in secret; and your Father who sees in secret will reward you openly." He recommends a simple mantra that can be internally recited any time of day: Yah-weh, Yah-weh, Yah-weh. It is the old Hebrew name for God. Do not say it in an uncaring or disrespectful manner and repeat the name silently within, for any conversation with the Divine is a deeply personal one. Once these two basic precepts are understood, then embrace the name with your heart, the place where all loving actions begin. Adding a steady breathing rhythm adds to the quality and depth of the experience. And be sure to talk to Him! The more you talk to God, the greater the experience and greater rewards will come your way. Trust the experience and trust the messages coming your way; trust, or faith if you will, is your only requirement. Remember, God cannot be explained; God cannot be defined; God can only be experienced!

So how do we experience God? It's quite simple really: be good, do good in everything you say and do, without exceptions!

Namaste!

Bibliography

Andrews, Ted. *Animal-Speak*. St. Paul: Llewellyn Publications, 1996.

Benes, Hans. "Boethius," Term Paper. Unpublished, 1995.

Benes, Hans. "The Beginning: Merging With the Light." Term Paper. Unpublished. 1993.

Boethius. The Consolation of Philosophy. Trans. V. E. Watts. London: Penguin Books, 1969.

Butterworth, Eric. *Spiritual Economics: The Principles and Process of True Prosperity*. Missouri: Unity Village, 2001.

Capo, Christa. Telephone interview. 22 Apr. 1993.

Emery, Eugene. "On the Brink of Death." <u>Providence Journal-Bulletin</u> March 23, 1986: 7-15.

Ferrini, Paul. *Love Without Conditions*. United States of America: Paul Ferrini, 1994 Ferrini, Paul. *The Laws of Love*. Greenfield: Heartways Press, 2004.

Freke, Timothy and Gandy, Peter. *Jesus and the Lost Goddess*. New York: Three Rivers Press, 2001.

Goddard, Neville. *The Power of Imagination*, The Neville Goddard Treasury. New York: TarcherPerigee, 2015.

Hawkins, David. *Power vs. Force*. Sedona: Veritas Publishing, 2012.

Howe, Linda. *How to Read the Akashic Records*. Boulder: Sounds True, 2009.

Jung, Carl G. "Approaching the Unconscious." *Classics of Western Thought: The Modern World*. Ed. Edgar E. Knoebel. 4th. ed. Vol. 3. Orlando: Harcourt Brace Jovanovich, 1988

Kubler-Ross, Elizabeth. Death, the Final Stage of Growth. Englewood Cliffs: Prentice- Hall, 1975.

Kubler-Ross, Elizabeth. *On Death and Dying*. New York: MacMillan, 1969.

Ladinsky, Daniel, translator. *Love Poems from God*. New York: Penguin Group, 2002.

Lifton, Robert. *Living and Dying*. New York: Praeger, 1974.

Levi. *The Aquarian Gospel of Jesus the Christ*. Marina del Rey: DeVorss and Company, 1997.

Lucretius. *The Nature of Things*. Trans. Frank O. Copley. New York: W.W. Norton and Company, 1977.

Marx, Karl. *The Communist Manifesto*. Chicago: Pluto Press. 1996.

Maxwell, Neal A. "Patience," Ensign, October 1980, p. 31.

Michael, Todd. *The Evolution Angel*. New York: Penguin Group. 2008. Morse, Melvin. Closer to the Light. New York: Ivy, 1990.

O'Leary, Donald. Telephone interview. 23 Apr. 1993.

Richelieu, Frank F. *The Art of Being Yourself*. Golden: Science of Mind Publishing,1992.

Roth, Patti. "Life After Near Death." <u>Fort Lauderdale Sun Sentinel</u> October 29,1984: 1C-4C.

Sagan, Carl. *Cosmos*. New York: Ballantine Books. 1980.

Spirit. Meditative messages to Hans Benes. Various dates.

St. Augustine. *The Confessions of St. Augustine.* Trans. Rex Warner. New York: Penguin Books, 1963.

Starcke, Walter. *The Third Appearance*. Boerne: Guadalupe Press, 2004.

Stewart, P. Raymond. *Living as God*: Healing the Separation. Vancouver: Namaste Publishing, 2004.

The Holy Bible: King James Version. Dallas: Brown Books Publishing, 2004.

The Urantia Book. (1955). Urantia Foundation.

Von Goethe, Johann Wolfgang. "Faust." *Classics of Western*

Thought: The Modern World. Ed. Edgar E. Knoebel. 4th. ed. Vol. 3. Orlando: Harcourt Brace Jovanovich, 1988.

Walsh, Neale Donald. *Conversations With God, Book 1*. New York. G.P Putnam's Sons, 1996.

Wilson, Ian. *The After Death Ex perience*. London: Sidgwick and Jackson, 1987.

Zauner, Phyllis. "Puzzling Visions of the Near-Dead." <u>American Legion</u> May 1982: 20-46.

Web Sites:

Carlton, Angel. "How to Navigate the 6 Stages of Transformation and Live Your destined Life." https://www.johnhuntpublishing.com/blogs/changemakers/the-six-stages-of- transformation/.

Chaudron, Marcel. "Change vs. Transformation." http://rocknchange.com/change-vs- transformation/.

Cherry, Kendra. "The 6 Stages of Behavior Change." https://www.verywellmind.com/the- stages-of-change-2794868

Social Media Links

Join me as we continue to explore the God within us all. Join me as we continue the search for who we really are. There is no greater purpose in our lives than to awaken to our spiritual roots and to share the experience with our brothers and sisters. Let's do good and be good in everything we say and do, without exception! "Change your thoughts...change the world." (Norman Vincent Peale)

The God Dichotomy Web Site:

https://www.thegoddichotomy.com/

My Personal Facebook Page:

https://www.facebook.com/hans.benes.3/

The God Dichotomy Youtube Channel:

https://www.youtube.com/channel/UCS3Fvx78lZg3iuCjWKDWwhg

The God Dichotomy Instagram Page:

https://www.instagram.com/thegoddichotomy/